The Tripoint

Julia Banasikowski Weir

This is a work of fiction. Apart from public figures, any resemblance of the characters to real people, either living or deceased, is coincidental. Space, time, and the opinions of public figures expressed in this novel have been rearranged for the convenience of this book. The story is loosely based on true events, but the plot and suggestion that the characters had influence on these true events is entirely fictitious.

To contact the author, please visit her website at

juliasweir.wordpress.com

Or follow her on Instagram **@jsweir_writes**

For Kristian. *Vive la résistance.*

Preface

I was raised in a small corner of Minneapolis called Northeast before it became the lovable arts district of the Twin Cities where all twenty-somethings wanted to live. Northeast was still reminiscent of the 1950s and 1960s with either a windowless bar or magnificent church on every street corner. The area had long been home to the local Eastern European community and housed our food market, Polish Saturday School, and parish. Most of my childhood took place in this trifecta of sites that ended up shaping my cultural, academic, and spiritual life.

My upbringing was shaped by a loving, closely knit, immigrant family that would also be considered today to be, among other things, hardass. The older generations came to this country to give their children better opportunities and instilled in me and my sister a strong love of family, heritage, and faith. At the same time, they had high expectations of us and ran a tight ship. If I came home from school with an A- grade on a project, my parents would ask why I didn't get an A. But this kind of upbringing was completely understandable, considering my family's background. I suppose when you're surrounded by generations of ancestors who survived the hardships of famines, wars, concentration camps, communism, displacement, and immigration, you come out a little more appreciative and a lot more disciplined.

At the head of this regimented family were my grandparents. My dad's mother, Zofia Banasikowski, had been prisoner to multiple Nazi concentration camps and other forced labor arrangements during World War II (which is a story in itself for a different book). My dad's father, Edmund Banasikowski, was a colonel in the Polish Home Army. My grandfather ultimately served as the model for Henryk Sosna, the grandfather of the main character of *The Tripoint*. Although this book begins with Henryk Sosna's funeral, he becomes as influential of a character as Joanna, his granddaughter. He communicates with her from the past through his writing and helps her decrypt his war secrets pursued by a menacing Russian enemy in an international chase for the truth.

I based Henryk Sosna's biography, told by Joanna in her eulogy at his funeral, off my grandfather's life. As she orates:

He was born into a military family on April 3, 1914, in Siedlce, Poland. He joined the School of Infantry Cadets in Komorowo, located in the Mazowiecki Voivodeship. In 1939, before the Nazi invasion of Poland, he rose to the rank of lieutenant.

After the war, my grandfather was considered a Damned Soldier (*żołnierz wyklęty*) by the newly instated communist regime. If found by the communists, he would have been arrested and perhaps even tortured and killed. He escaped Poland on a barge to a refugee camp in Sweden, where he met and married my grandmother. They eventually immigrated to Milwaukee, Wisconsin, where they raised my aunt and father.

During his time in the United States, my grandfather was an anticommunist activist, meeting frequently with politicians, appearing on radio broadcasts, and writing almost incessantly about fighting for a free Poland. As Joanna continues in her eulogy:

They started a new life, but for them, the war was not yet over. My grandfather was a member of the

Polish American Congress for 17 years, a news correspondent for Radio Free Europe, and the president of the Polish Combatants Association. He met with congressmen and U.S. presidents to advocate for the Polish cause and raise morale to defeat communism from abroad. He only returned to Poland after communism had fallen. He kissed the ground when his plane landed at the Chopin International Airport.

In April 2010, following my grandfather's death, a most bizarre series of events took place in Poland. Just days after my grandfather's funeral, a plane carrying the President and First Lady of Poland crashed in Russia, killing them along with almost one hundred other representatives of the Polish government. The ensemble of politicians was traveling to the town of Smoleńsk, Russia to commemorate the 70th anniversary of the Katyń Massacre, a war crime perpetrated by the Soviets in 1940 on over 20,000 Polish officers, priests, professors, and intelligentsia. The plane crashed in the same Russian forest where most of the massacre had taken place decades before.

The reported cause of the disaster was the poor weather conditions in the area; the pilot reportedly couldn't see the terrain due to the thick fog and flew the plane into the trees, missing the runway. The eerie coincidence of the plane crash and the anniversary of the massacre, however, immediately raised a serious question on a global stage. Was this a coordinated attack on the Polish government by the Russians?

Formal investigations were completed by a Russian committee with international cooperation. At the time I am writing *The Tripoint*, over 10 years have passed since the disaster took place and all findings support that the plane crashed due to pilot error. This was not, as some skeptics believed, an attempt by Russia to resurrect their sphere of influence over Poland and to overthrow the Polish government by assassinating their president and several other politicians. Nothing sinister had taken place.

The week of events, starting with my grandfather's death and ending with the plane crash in Smoleńsk, was one of the most unusual times in my life. The emotions of the funeral, followed closely by the shocking catastrophe in the Russian woods, spurred my imagination. My grandfather was a military hero who had spent most of his life fighting against the Soviets during World War II and the Cold War. Would it have been believable that his legacy had some kind of connection to this plane crash so soon after his death?

I'd say that *The Tripoint* is inspired by true events, but I don't want to mislead my readers. My grandfather was a real person and influenced the character Henryk Sosna, but the lover that Sosna had during World War II and the secrets he wrote into his war memoir were just figments of my imagination. Likewise, the 2010 plane crash in Smoleńsk was a real event, but to say it was an orchestrated attack on the Polish government would be erroneous to the investigations' findings.

Instead, I'll say that *The Tripoint* is inspired by true honor, with true people and true events serving as the platform on which I build a story. I hope you enjoy this tour through 20th century history, sampling from my childhood, my family's experience during the war, and what I've learned from both the living and the dead.

„Jeśli zapomnę o Nich – ty Boże na niebie zapomnij o mnie!"

"Should I forget them – may You, God in Heaven, forget me!"

Adam Mickiewicz, *Dziady*

1

My grandfather always hated what Americans liked to call celebrations of life. He said that in place of funerals, they force you out of natural melancholy and into this artificial showcase of joy. He despised that people wanted so badly to escape from grief, even though it was as commonplace to the human heart as happiness. We could never live in an eternal state of bliss. That was not what our time on earth was for.

Whatever my thoughts on life after death, I agreed with him on this concept of one's final commemoration. Perhaps it was my immigrant upbringing in a culture that so passionately embraced death, but I hated the spectacle as well. Some pictures in a cheap slideshow of the deceased, overlaid with "What a Wonderful World" by Louis Armstrong, with guests chattering merrily among themselves as the ashes of a person who once lived laid off to the side. The remains would be preferably cremated, for Americans. *God forbid the children are traumatized by an open-casket wake!* My grandfather thought the people who made those remarks were just protecting themselves. They hadn't accepted their own mortality yet, and they refused to wallow in that of anyone else.

And so, naturally, my grandfather was not cremated. He wanted to be buried as a whole, dressed in the forest green wool military uniform, which he wore when he came to this country during the Cold War. Although few came to his funeral, every attendee admired his layers of metal badges affixed to his left breast as they passed his open casket, crossing themselves. On top of the badges lay his most prized award – the Virtuti Militari. Standing over his body at the wake in the church hall, I still hadn't decided whether I should steal the badge off his chest before they closed the casket and keep it as the single family possession I could share with others. But share with whom? Even after my parents died, I donated all their clothes and belongings to the local Salvation Army. I didn't need them, and I certainly didn't have any relatives who might need them, either. The usher closed the casket sealing away my grandfather, Virtuti Militari badge and all.

The procession to the front of the church was short and mournful, just as my grandfather, whom I called Dziadek, would have wanted it. It was easy to plan this funeral because he was so much like me – unambiguous, objective, and rarely sentimental. We knew what was important in our lives, and the rest was cut out.

It was even easier to plan Dziadek's funeral than the one for my parents. I was 20 years old and studying at university abroad when the school called me to the administrative offices and informed me that my parents had both perished in a car accident. The simultaneous deaths were sudden and shocking, of course, but that didn't mean they hadn't planned every part of their funeral. The expectations my parents had were elaborate. They wanted a full choir accompanied by a specific organist; they expected an *uczta* of food, all homemade, spanning several tables at the luncheon; they arranged which priests should be flown in to Chicago from Poland for the Mass; and they knew which suit and dress they would be buried in. They didn't need to tell me any of the details prior to their unexpected death. They had already meticulously spelled everything out in their will years before. I would have done my own funeral differently, but I carried out their every written command. It is the last act of respect one could do for the dead.

Dziadek did not have a will because everything would be inevitably inherited by me, his single surviving relative, the only daughter of his only son. I didn't mind the lack of guidance. I knew exactly how he'd want this final occasion to look.

After the procession into the Church of the Holy Trinity, familiarly called Trójcowo by Polish immigrants in the Chicago area, there was a full Mass in our native tongue. We passed under the triangular portico, supported by Corinthian columns, and made our way into the Cathedral-style Romanesque sanctuary. The walls and altars were adorned with paintings of the Black Madonna, stained-glass windows, and statues of iconic saints that every Pole knew. The church was almost a century and a half old, built by immigrants with their own hands. Every time I entered it, I reminded myself that there were few things in this melting pot country that were as well-preserved as this parish in which I had been raised. As my cousin once told me, there are functioning toilets in Poland that are older than even the most antiquated American churches.

As we were seated for the Liturgy of the Word, I lowered myself down into the first pew next to Dziadek's best friend. He was formally known as Lieutenant Zygmunt Łowicki, but he was like an uncle to me, and so I called him by that title, Wujek, my entire life. His wife, Helena, sat on his right. The three of us made up what remained of Dziadek's closest milieu.

Following the Liturgy of the Eucharist, it was finally my turn to say the eulogy. I had written it out and practiced it once that same morning, so it was somber, but not emotional, for me. Few things made me emotional. It seemed that not even death moved me in that way anymore.

I walked up to the ambo to the right of the altar and laid my papers out in front of me. I looked over the pews and accounted for the usual suspects at a Trójcowo funeral Mass: close family and friends in the first row, followed by a few scattered elderly parishioners who read about the funeral in the bulletin the Sunday before. The ushers from the funeral home stood in the back of the church.

But there was one person, a blond, younger man, who sat behind everyone. He was about my age, so I ran through a short list of acquaintances that I or my family had made in the past which might connect this man to my grandfather. I registered zero results in my memory and proceeded with the eulogy.

"Today we bid farewell to Colonel Henryk Jerzy Sosna," I began in Polish. "He was a family man, a friend, an expert card player when he had his fill of vodka, an immigrant with a gritty work ethic, and a national hero. I am sure many of you admired his medals during the wake. As a child, I remember he could not part with them. They hung in his bedroom over his desk, where he spent years writing his war memoir. Today, they accompany him to his grave as we honorably bury this great defender of Poland.

"Most of you know his life, but I can't imagine standing here in his church, surrounded by his spiritual presence, and omitting his accomplishments from today's events. He was born into a military family on April 3, 1914, in Siedlce, Poland. He joined the School of Infantry Cadets in Komorowo, located in the Mazowiecki Voivodeship. In 1939, before the Nazi invasion of Poland, he rose to the rank of lieutenant. This was a monumental year, not only for his nation and the world, but for his personal life. This was the year that he met and married the love of his life, his treasure, my grandmother, Magda. Though thrown about the country by their wartime fate, they would eventually reunite.

"After the September Campaign, he spent two years in the underground until he was named commander of the Wachlarz armed organization, which operated primarily in Vilnius. After his first arrest by the Soviet NKVD, he escaped to Warsaw, and spent the rest of the war fighting both the Nazis and the Soviets in the capital of Poland and in Vilnius. My grandparents reunited at the site of the church where they had been married and, although the church had been destroyed during the 1944 Warsaw Uprising, they still remembered the street. My grandfather waited on the block, standing in the rubble of the city, every single day after the war ended until my grandmother arrived. They knew if God could reunite them despite the hardship they had each faced in the war, they could do anything together."

I paused to acknowledge the sniffles coming from the parishioners sitting behind Wujek. Even Helena was wiping a tear from her eye, recalling her dear friend, Magda, who had died almost a decade ago, missing the most difficult years of Dziadek's battle with Alzheimer's disease. Wujek and the blond man in the back were solemn. After my quick assessment of the emotional state of the funeral guests, I continued.

"After the war formally ended in Europe, Henryk was hunted by the communists because of his activity in Wachlarz, so my grandparents escaped communist Poland in 1946 and fled to America. They started a new life, but for them, the war was not yet over. My grandfather was a member of the Polish American Congress for 17 years, a news correspondent for Radio Free Europe, and the president of the Polish Combatants Association. He met with congressmen and U.S. presidents to advocate for the Polish cause and raise morale to defeat communism from abroad. He only returned to Poland after communism had fallen. He kissed the ground when his plane landed at the Chopin International Airport."

I paused, forcing down the lump in my throat. I had promised myself to speak without any vulnerability at this funeral, but the image of my grandfather, who had been away from his homeland for over 40 years, finally coming back to his freed country struck a sensitive chord in me.

"His body is gone, but his spirit remains. In fact, he left behind perhaps the greatest gift he could offer, his most notable achievement, his war memoir. During the 1980s, he wrote and published *On the Call to Vilnius*. He received the literary award from the Union of Polish Writers Abroad for his composition, which is considered today to be the basic textbook for understanding the history of the Polish underground during World War II. His words, quite literally, are still with us."

I pulled out a sealed envelope, which I had been storing curiously since his death a few days before, from behind my eulogy papers.

"My grandfather asked that this be read at his funeral. He wrote this years ago, before the heavy onset of his Alzheimer's. I think he knew his mind was leaving him, and he wanted to preserve the beauty of the words he once knew to write so eloquently. I'd like to open this letter now, for the first time, and leave you with his final words.

"*Dearest friends and family,*

"*I've now left this world, as we all will. I trust I went to my heavenly home, and I trust I will meet you* all there one day. I am with my wife, Magda; with my son, Radek; and with God.

"I was not afraid to die. The war taught me that death is as sure as life. I wasn't afraid to die because I've left all I can on this earth. With my war memoir, I want to be a bridge between what lives and what has passed. With it, I commemorate those who died before me, the honorable warriors with whom I had the privilege of sharing the most eventful years of my life. And I hope to teach others in the future about what we experienced, where we went, and what we fought for.

"Radek, my son, you were like a mirror of my younger self. In you, I saw the future of Polish emigres, and you pushed me to fight for a free Poland so you could indulge in its gifts and beauty, as I had done as a young man.

"Magda, you were the key to my life. With you, I could unlock all things, escape from all things, see all things, and love all things.

"Joanna, my doll, my granddaughter, you are my hope. You can do anything you set your mind to, child. You are ambition itself, and I am proud of the woman you have become. You now carry this family.

"My words and my love are with all of you. I've done my best to live my life for God, Country, and Honor. My final prayer is that, with my life, I've led by example for you to do the same.

"*Gloria victis.*"

I folded the letter, slid the papers off the ambo, and returned to my pew. I sat down next to Wujek as he placed his old, calloused hand on top of mine. With just his touch, I knew he felt the same way I did: the honor was ours to have known this man. Our clasped hands rested on my knee until it was time to stand again and proceed out of the church with the casket to the hearse parked outside.

Following the burial at the nearby cemetery, which we were eager to finish considering the cold drizzle wisping across our faces, I invited everyone to Dziadek's favorite Polish restaurant in Chicago. The restaurant was, in fact, a refined one. Dziadek had good taste and knew to forgo the kitschy northside bars that turned Polish culture and cuisine into a caricature, suitable for a tourist, but not for an actual citizen of the same homeland.

The restaurant served his favorite meal, the steak tartare, complete with a raw egg yolk on top of the mound of meat. I had ordered a plate of it for every guest ahead of time as an homage to him. When we arrived, we were seated at two tables, one for close friends and family, the other for church parishioners and miscellaneous guests.

A few more people who were not at the church trickled into the restaurant. I greeted them respectfully and pretended not to mind their excuses of why they could not attend the funeral. I was not a practicing Catholic anymore, either, but it was still a moral obligation to honor the dead in the way they wanted to be remembered.

By the time Wujek started pouring everyone shots of vodka from the bottles of Chopin that rested in the ice bucket stands beside each table, we had already asked the waiters to prepare a third table for our abundance of guests. The ambiance shifted from quiet and solemn to vivacious and jovial. Wujek was leading toasts and ordering drinks and appetizers, one right after the other. Eventually, the wooden carts on which the steak tartare would be prepared were rolled out, accompanied by an ensemble of cooks who wielded sharp kitchen knives and an array of herbs for the dish.

Gatherings like this came with a heavy wave of nostalgia for my childhood. It seemed my young social life mirrored that of my parents: I went wherever they went, which was always to other Polish immigrant homes. While other children my age would go to the basement to play at those parties, I would make myself a plate of food and sit in a corner, unnoticed, listening to the adult conversations around me. My parents and their friends spoke of history, politics, art, sports, faith. I learned more in the corners of those rooms than I ever did in the classroom of my grade school.

The atmosphere of the funeral reception was no different. Wujek started talking about his involvement with the Solidarity movement and the Gdańsk shipyards. My grandfather's former neighbor, an Italian immigrant named Sergio, explained how my grandfather would interrupt conversations at the Sosna house to receive phone calls from Ronald Reagan. One of the parishioners told stories about the concentration camps she was held in and what the liberation by the Swedish Red Cross was like.

These stories swirled around me throughout the evening until we realized the restaurant was beginning to close. Even more unfortunate than the restaurant closure, however, was the news that our three tables had drunk through the establishment's entire stock of Chopin vodka that night. With that information, I closed the party's tab, signaling the end of the gathering. Dziadek would have been pleased.

I stood up from my seat with Wujek and Helena, pulling on my fur mink coat over my black dress while turning my phone on to call a cab. Before I could navigate to my contacts, I saw someone approach me from the corner of my eye.

"Miss Sosna?"

I looked up to see the blond man from the funeral standing in front of me. I glanced around, noticing most of the guests had left. In his subtle, archaic elegance, Wujek was putting on his fedora at the entrance of the restaurant while Helena blew me a kiss goodbye from across the room.

"Hello," I responded, turning back to the man.

"My name is Kacper Tomczyk, I wanted to introduce myself. I wanted to thank you for the evening. I was sitting at the other table, we were all listening to the stories from your side, and it was such a moving night." I extended my hand toward him, forgetting the common Polish greeting gesture, as he leaned in to kiss each of my cheeks. Normally I would have been revolted by such a forward expression upon first encounter, but between the persuasion of the vodka and his stunning blue eyes, I did not mind at all.

"Thank you for joining us and helping commemorate my grandfather. May I ask, do I know you?"

"Probably not," he flashed a beautiful, white smile and turned his bashful gaze away. "I saw your grandfather's obituary in the Chicago Tribune. He was an extraordinary man. I read his war memoir while I was studying military history at the Jagiellonian University in Kraków during my undergraduate studies. I'm now at the University of Chicago for my PhD."

"That makes sense," I nodded, smiling back at him. "He was a wonderful man. I am fortunate to have known him, to have been molded by his life."

"I can't imagine the influence he must have had on you."

"You're from Poland, then?" I asked, hoping he was not in a rush to leave.

"Yes, from Wrocław, originally. I've only been in the States for two years." His English grammar was perfect, but he spoke with a slight accent. His smooth voice nearly sent me into a trance.

"And how are you liking Chicago?" I pulled on my leather gloves.

"It's a big city, it's impressive. But sometimes I miss the quiet you could so easily find in Poland, at a pub or a short drive away from town. The girls are different here, too." He left his statement open for interpretation, but the look he gave me indicated I might have been the good kind of different.

"I know what you mean. I miss it, too. Poland, not the girls," I smiled at the ludicrousness of my own clarification.

"Tonight was the first night that felt..." Kacper looked around the restaurant in search of a word. "Familiar. The people were genuine and interesting, not superficial and boring."

"If you're in academia, I'm sure you have no shortage of genuine, interesting people."

"You'd be surprised, Miss Sosna."

"You can call me Joanna."

"Joanna," he smiled again, looking me straight in the eye. His gaze was soft, though, and made my heart beat even louder. "I know it's late, Joanna, but I was wondering if you'd like to have a drink with me?"

"Oh, since we drank this place dry?" My comment made him laugh out loud.

"You could say that. There's another bar just down the block. I can assure you they still have Chopin and, if not, Belvedere, if you can settle. Join me for a drink?" I looked over my shoulder to ensure that Wujek and Helena had left the restaurant. The entire building was empty, other than the residual night staff who began mopping the floors.

"One drink," I agreed. I absorbed one last long look, and then turned towards the door of the restaurant, into the night with the unexplored man I had met the day of my grandfather's funeral.

2

I realized that talking with Kacper was as effortless as breathing. He knew everything that I did about our country of origin and its history, and more. He had a degree in history and my career was in finance after studying mathematics, but I kept up with him on 20th century European military and political events. We agreed that Poland's first democratically elected president after the fall of communism, Lech Wałęsa, was considered too much of a hero on the international stage when, in fact, he sold out many of his dissident colleagues to the communists. We understood that Russia should still be held accountable for the 1940 Katyń Massacre, even 70 years after the event. Kacper even went on a soliloquy about why Poland is right to remain economically independent of the European Union and hang on to its national currency instead of conforming to the eurozone. I was almost alarmed that our views aligned so much, considering his liberal academic background. I thought the only living person in Chicago who shared the same opinions as me was Wujek.

The bar Kacper selected was a modern hole in the wall, a rustic shift from the elegance of the restaurant we had left. The exposed brick and cement floors gave it a worn appearance, but the idiosyncratic cocktails, topped with turmeric-flavored whipped egg whites and smoke water with pine needles, confirmed for me that Kacper had picked a cultivated place.

"I'll end with a vodka tonic, and then I should be getting home," I informed the waiter, who came to take our final drink order before the bar closed.

"I'll do the same." The waiter nodded and returned moments later with our refreshments.

"How did your grandfather die?" Kacper asked, taking a sip of his drink. My head felt light, but I grounded myself in this first of what, I presumed, would be a series of more personal questions.

"He had Alzheimer's, but in the end, it was a stroke that took his life."

"And he lived here in Chicago as well?"

"Yes, on the southside, actually. In a small apartment." *Until he was moved to a retirement home half a year ago, and then hospice.* I knew what information to withhold in a first encounter.

"It must have been very sudden for you, despite his illness."

"Yes, very." *Not at all, actually. I had expected this for months.*

"I am so sorry for your loss. Forgive my forward offer, but I didn't see many people at the funeral today. Would you need any help sorting through his things in the coming days? I can imagine there are loads of documents you need to page through and archive for yourself and your family."

I forced myself to suppress the flinch I would have normally given at the suggestion and instead took another drink of the vodka tonic, holding his gaze.

"You know," I started, looking at him doe-eyed and setting my glass down. "Why don't you come over tomorrow, later in the morning? I'd love to see you again." I reached across the table to test the waters. He leaned forward, subtly enthusiastic, and took my hand.

"I'd love to."

"Perfect." I pulled my hand away, reaching for my glass. I took one last sip, staring into his eyes the entire time.

"May I walk you home, Miss Sosna?"

"I've been telling you the whole night, it's Joanna. But yes, please."

We entered the brisk night again, called a cab, and arrived at the building of my condo located in the Gold Coast neighborhood 20 minutes later. The highways were empty except for the lost souls returning home from late night clubs with the questionable acquaintances they met that night. I had my own.

I swiped into the building with my key card, punched the code to my penthouse, and rode the elevator to the top floor with Kacper at my side. He looked inquisitively around every hallway we walked until I unlocked the door to my home.

Kacper had no problem keeping pace with my confidence and followed me into the condo, closing the door behind him.

"Another vodka tonic?" I offered as I slipped the mink off my shoulders and threw it on the Chesterfield couch facing the wood-burning fireplace. The room was dimly lit at 2:00 in the morning, making the surrounding city lights appear exceptionally radiant. I made my way to the bar, pulled out two glasses, and reached for the vodka in the freezer below the counter.

"Mmm..." He hummed deliciously, taking off his own coat. I loved his every sound.

I focused on mixing the two drinks as I felt him approach me. His hands wandered to my hips, and then turned me around, pressing my lower back into the edge of the bar behind me. He kissed me, first softly, and then more firmly, as his hands made their way to my chest. Mirroring his gesture, I grazed my hands across the sides of his body and then to the line of silver buttons down the front of his shirt. My hands kept roaming his chest until my fingertips grazed over something that felt like a cord under his shirt.

As if he could read my mind that something was wrong, Kacper pulled away slightly.

"Will you save me that drink for tomorrow?" He whispered between kisses. He was almost irresistible, feigning a gentleman.

"A morning drinker?" I made sure to keep up my act as if I hadn't felt anything out of the ordinary.

"Only if you are."

"I might even make it two," I smiled as he leaned away from me. "Come by at 10 tomorrow morning. I'll have breakfast waiting, if you're good."

"You're lucky I was good tonight."

Kacper stepped back and walked towards the coat he laid on the couch next to mine. I met him at the door, gave him a kiss goodnight, and watched as he made his way down the hallway to the elevator bank. I leaned against the door frame, doing my best to appear helplessly in love, until he stepped into the lift.

As soon as he was out of sight, I shut the door and locked the dead bolt. On my way to the panoramic window overlooking Lake Michigan, I picked up the vodka tonic I had prepared at the counter and tossed the other glass carelessly into the bar sink. When I got to the window, I glanced down the 30 floors to the street level and waited for Kacper to cross the street. I kicked off my heels into a corner and pulled my hair out of its tight bun as I watched him get into a cab and drive away.

Freedom.

Drink in hand, I dropped myself into the Chesterfield against the lush pillows lining the couch and reached into the pocket of my fur coat for my phone. I typed out the phone number I had memorized years ago, one that I purposely omitted from my contacts list, and wrote the text I had been taught to use only in cases where I was absolutely confident that I needed assistance.

"*Akcja W.*"

I hit the send button. Seconds later, my phone vibrated with the expected cryptic response from the same number.

"*Gloria victis.*" And the meeting was confirmed.

I leaned forward out of the couch and unstrapped the Velcro that held my nine-millimeter Beretta in its hiding place underneath the wooden coffee table. I set it gently on the surface in front of me. In the stark moonlight reflecting off the lake through the window, the gun was the only item in the spotlight. I admired the piece in between sips of the vodka tonic and recalled when Dziadek took me to the gun shop to buy it when I was 18 years old. It was my first Beretta, my secret sister. I hadn't needed to use it yet, but I knew what to do with it if the time came. Dziadek was gone, Wujek was old, and I was alone.

I downed the last of the drink and lifted my uncoordinated self off of the couch, taking the Beretta with me. I undressed as I made my way to my room, leaving pieces of clothing along the hallway behind me, and then collapsed onto my bed into an immediate, unbothered slumber.

3

A few hours later, I was awake again, not out of necessity, but out of old habit. My grandfather lived for the morning and thought the day was useless after noon. For him, the early bird didn't get the worm, but rather the enemy. I did not have enemies, but better safe than sorry.

My television automatically turned on at 5:00 as my alarm clock and was set to broadcast the live noon news special from Warsaw every day. At least if I got up this early, I could catch up on what had happened in Poland the first half of the day and then be awake concurrently with the people of both countries of my dual citizenship.

The familiar, rapid voice of the news reporter boomed from the living room as I rolled out of bed and headed towards the espresso machine in the kitchen. The condo was as dark as it had been when Kacper had dropped me off, but within the hour, the subtlest hint of the rising sun tinted the horizon above the lake pink. Soon the façade of the entire city was painted golden with the morning palette.

The espresso reinvigorated all my senses, which had been dulled from the vodka the night before, and allowed me to focus on that morning's planned task: research. I searched the Internet for every website, publication, and social media account that gave me any kind of information about Kacper Tomczyk. A pseudonym would have been too obvious for him to use; if I googled his name and nothing came up, it would have been an even bigger red flag. His résumé was impressive, so it wasn't difficult to find the results I was looking for.

"Graduated *magna cum laude* from Jagiellonian in 2006, completed a two-year practicum with the Institute of National Remembrance in Warsaw, enrolled in the doctorate program at the University of Chicago..." I read his credentials aloud to myself, confirming all the information he shared with me the night before.

I checked the Patek Phillipe I had left on my counter after work on Friday – 6:15. I still had time to work out, shower, and change before the meeting at 8:00, and I needed to be back in time for Kacper's expected return later that morning. Realizing the tight schedule, I quickly took an almond biscotti from the glass jar on the kitchen counter and pulled on my workout clothes. I descended 30 floors of the stairwell as my warm-up while swaddling each hand into its cotton-polyester blend wrap with the assistance of my teeth. By the time I arrived at the gym, I was ready for my daily boxing regimen. The routine had been beaten into me years before and, as Dziadek always said, the best habits were built at sunrise.

An hour and a half later, I was smearing on red lipstick in the elevator and getting into my Audi. I drove back through the northside, retracing my footsteps from the night before, and parked across the street from Trójcowo, just as a flock of parishioners were exiting the church. I passed through the small crowd of men, women, and children chattering among themselves in Polish and entered the quiet sanctuary. At the end of the aisle, as if he hadn't moved from my grandfather's funeral the day before, Wujek sat alone in the first pew, staring at the crucifix hanging above the altar. I bowed in the direction of the tabernacle before seating myself into the pew next to him.

"You know, you had your baptism here. Your first communion, your confirmation... I've witnessed all the momentous occasions you've had so far in your life," Wujek began.

"You're still so sentimental about this place."

"You don't come here anymore? I don't see you at Sunday Mass. It's probably been years since you've been here, other than the funeral yesterday."

"I say a Hail Mary in the morning and hope God forgives me when I die." I remained focused on the altar as Wujek was. The smell of the incense still lingered in the air from the celebration of the Mass and brought back memories from my early years, exploring the church cellar and watching my friends from my Polish Saturday School class serve as altar boys.

"Your grandfather was at every momentous occasion of your life, too. And he was at every important event in my life, most significantly, the day he saved my life."

"He went into the prison after you were arrested during the war to drag you out of there himself, didn't he?"

"Not just any prison. I was held in Pawiak, my child. Tortured for weeks to leak information about Akcja W, about Wachlarz, but I didn't say a word. I didn't know how much longer I'd last, but he got himself arrested just in time. We both intentionally contracted typhus from this tiny little glass bottle of infected fabric he managed to smuggle into the prison, and he was the reason we were transferred to a different unit and eventually escaped."

"Those were the days, huh, Wujek?" I asked, attempting to lighten the mood. I wasn't there for a heartwarming family history lesson. Wujek ignored my comment, as he usually did when I said something sprightly.

"From then on, I vowed to give my life for him. After your father was born, and after you were born, I made that vow transferrable to both of you. Your grandfather is gone. Your parents are both gone. And now, all I have is you to protect." Wujek took my hand into his own on my lap. "You used the code I taught you when you were still a young girl, which means you needed to see me."

"I always thought it was silly that we set up an entire mobile phone number for the purpose of me contacting you in this one unlikely situation, but now I understand why we did so."

"The young always doubt the old until they themselves are wise enough to know their ways."

"Why did a man try to whisk me off my feet with a night on the town the very same day of my grandfather's funeral?"

"Was he handsome?" Wujek joked. I didn't need to look to know that the slightest smile spread across his time-worn, wrinkled face.

"He was wired." A pause between us indicated to me that the smile had vanished.

"What did you tell him about Henryk?"

"Nothing. I'm not naïve." Wujek took a deep breath and dropped my hand back in my lap. He crossed his arms over his chest, then uncrossed them, deciding it wasn't comfortable.

"Your grandfather had... *niedokończone sprawy*... how do you say... unfinished business, in Poland when he left after the war."

"*Mówmy po polsku*," I prompted him quietly to switch to our native tongue. "And keep your voice down. I know you're going deaf, but I can hear you, I'm sitting right here. Do you know what kind of business?"

"He didn't tell anyone what the matters related to," Wujek said, shaking his head. "Not even me. Forgive him for that. He didn't want to burden anyone else with whatever knowledge he had. He knew that if anyone would come looking for answers about the war, he wanted to be the first and only one to know that truth. That's how we operated in the underground. The less you knew, the less the enemy could scare out of you."

"How the hell am I supposed to know what this guy is looking for?"

"Who does he say he is?"

"His name is Kacper Tomczyk. He's a PhD student at the University of Chicago. Studied at Jagiellonian. Obviously knows loads about Wachlarz, we spent the entire night talking about their operations during the war. I looked him up this morning, he's legitimate."

"The timing is suspicious, yes. He was waiting for your grandfather to pass before he contacted you. And you're sure it was a wire?"

"If it was a crucifix necklace, it was the thickest and longest I've ever felt under a shirt. He was recording me. And then he offered to come over and help me sort through Dziadek's documents."

"Amateur," Wujek scoffed. "So, he's being paid by someone else. He doesn't do this by profession. What did you tell him?"

"I told him to come over later this morning."

"For an interrogation. Smart girl."

"What is he after, Wujek? You know I can defend myself, but if there's something in Dziadek's documents he's after, I wouldn't even know what to look for that's pertinent to someone that's still alive."

"After your grandfather sold the house and was moved to the hospice center, you took all his possessions to your condo, no?"

"They're all locked in a separate room. I haven't even gone through them since he died."

"Anything that had any historical or military worth was transferred to the Institute of National Remembrance in Warsaw. Destroy whatever you have at your condo. Your grandfather was emotionally attached to the things he left behind – letters, photographs – but if there's something buried in them that we don't know about, it's better that it doesn't exist."

"Then the only thing we'd have left to remember his war account by would be his memoir."

"Don't tell me you're sentimental about his shit, too, Joanna," Wujek gestured passionately with his hands through the air as he spoke. "It's been combed through by the greatest historians from around the world. There's nothing left for anyone there, and if something is hidden, it's best that it remains undisclosed."

"I'll burn it as soon as I get home."

"You should go now. Destroy it before he gets there."

Wujek grabbed at the back of the wooden pew in front of us and pulled himself up to stand. I followed, supporting him under his left arm and shuffling out of the pew into the aisle. He paused to bow towards the altar and then turned with me to walk to the back of the church.

As we stepped outside, he unraveled his arm from mine. I reached into my pocket for my cloves and lighter.

"What the hell are those?"

"Djarum Blacks. They're cloves. Want one?"

"I only smoke what I roll myself." I knew he'd be repulsed by the thought of anything that was purchased outside of the European Union or any concept that originated after the Cold War. If it didn't exist during World War II, or even postwar communism, it was a modernist idea he wanted no part in. He was like my grandfather – simple, routine, and remarkably predictable.

Wujek pulled out his cell phone, an archaic Nokia that could not have been manufactured any later than 2002. I rolled my eyes and turned away as he started typing in a phone number slowly with his pointer finger. Without seeing the digits, I already knew the person he was contacting.

"Please don't text Emil," I begged.

"What do you have against my grandson, remind me again?" Wujek's eyes remained glued attentively to the small green screen of his Nokia.

I hadn't seen Emil in years. We attended Polish Saturday School growing up on the northside of Chicago together. We were some of the only children at gatherings between the Łowicki and the Sosna families until we graduated from high school. Before graduation, we even traveled to and from Poland together when our parents signed us up for the same self-defense camps, held in the mountains. We attended the same six-week camp every summer for years, paid for entirely by our grandfathers, so they knew their grandchildren would be trained in a trusted military-like fashion. We learned everything together – survival in the wilderness, attacks and counterattacks, knife handling, martial arts, and shooting rifles and handguns. Emil would joke that he and I were like the Polish Bonnie and Clyde, and we could pursue any villain together.

Then he went to Oxford, and I went to the Sorbonne. An accomplished athlete and widely published academic in the area of history, he was attractive both physically and intellectually. Other women seemed to think so, too, considering he came back from college every winter break with a different girlfriend. There was never an opportunity for a relationship between us, much to our respective grandfather's dismay and, at this point, seeing him again would make me nervous for what could potentially happen. I had my career to focus on, and that was enough for me. I had no idea what he had to focus on, and I didn't want to raise any hopes that it might be me.

"Emil's going to come by your condo right now. Remember, burn everything. You should be on your way back," Wujek informed me. I took a deep drag of my sweet, black-papered cigarette to calm myself. *Emil doesn't have anything better to do this early on a Sunday morning? Shouldn't he be waking up next to some supermodel he picked up the night before?*

"Fine."

"Take care of yourself. I know you don't need me to do that."

"Or Emil."

"You two would make a good couple, Joanna. Don't scare him off."

"Thank you for your help, Wujek." I dropped my half-smoked cigarette to the ground and put it out with the toe of my shiny black shoe. I leaned into Wujek to kiss him goodbye, once on each cheek, and put my sunglasses on. I turned towards my car, every step taking me closer to the man whose very existence made me shed all assurance I had in myself and shake in the very heels I thought I put on this morning to make me feel poised.

4

I didn't have time to clean the condo upon my return that morning before a knock came at my door. I sighed as I opened the door to find the strapping, clean-cut man I had last seen a few Christmases ago.

"Joanna..." He looked me up and down, his gaze lingering in the places that had developed most since we last met. I hadn't taken my Louboutins off since arriving, but even in heels, he was still several inches taller than me.

"Emil," I greeted him with a kiss on each cheek. We had this nonchalance about each other because of our shared childhood. Even though I was overwhelmed in seeing him again, I had to maintain the same composure he showed. He was my equal, I had to remind myself. No need to get giddy around him and letting his head get big.

"Grandfather told me to show up as soon as I could. What's happening?"

"Make yourself a coffee and meet me in the spare bedroom," I said, remembering the haste with which we had to move.

"What's the hurry? I see the Beretta's out, so something must have happened." Emil yelled from the kitchen as I walked down the hall to the locked bedroom, picking up my clothes along the way. I threw them in the laundry hamper before unlocking the door to the other room.

"You know if you were called here, there's obviously going to be a hurry. You're not here for mimosas, Emil," I shouted back.

"Aye, aye, captain," he said quietly and sarcastically in the kitchen.

"Tell me the time."

"9:00."

"Shit. We have an hour. Can you make a fire, please?"

"It's April and 60 degrees outside, Joanna," he responded, though I heard him walking across the living room obediently and shuffling around the logs and cardboard near the fireplace.

"When the fire gets going, come in here and help me sort through this, I'll explain when you get in here."

Minutes later, Emil appeared at the door of the spare bedroom with his cup of espresso. He chose to drink from my favorite Tiffany espresso set, the tiny clear glass sitting atop its saucer. He took in the sight of me kneeling over half a dozen suitcases full of old papers spread out across the wooden floor.

"Good lord. I didn't know I was being invited to a book burning."

"Even better – a military document conflagration. Take these." I handed him a stack of papers and motioned for him to leave the bedroom and dispose of the documents in the fireplace. We worked in this assembly line, me as the paper handler and him as the deliverer, while I recounted the prior night to him.

"You're sure it was a wire?"

"Your grandfather asked me the same thing this morning. Of course I'm sure."

"Smart of you to invite him back, to invite him over at all last night."

"Why weren't you at the funeral?" I changed the subject, asking the question that had been on my mind since the procession the day before. I heard him sigh.

"I'm sorry, Joanna. I was flying back from Boston yesterday. I couldn't make it."

"Not even to the reception?" I handed him another stack of papers.

"I don't have an excuse. I'm sorry, and I'm sorry for your loss."

"Your grandfather's presence doesn't account for your own, you know. He may be the patriarch of your family, but you count just as much." Maybe I was acting emotionally, but I knew honor meant the same to Emil as it did to me. He was just lazy about it, which both of our grandfathers would have despised.

"I'm sorry," he repeated himself again, and knelt next to me on the floor. He took my wrist into his hand to pause my automated activity of gathering papers. I looked him in the eye for the first time that morning.

"Apology accepted."

We spent the next half hour catching up on each other's lives, discussing careers, projects, and travel both of us had spent the last few years doing. Through conversation, the stacks of paper finally began dwindling.

"We only have 10 minutes left. Drag these suitcases to the living room, let's finish in there. Make sure you've taken every single document from this room. Are you sure you don't have any keepsake boxes or other mementos from him?" Emil asked.

"I'm positive. I don't keep anything from my family. You know that."

"Yeah, and your condo is just as vacant. No personality whatsoever."

"What do you expect, a massive white eagle painted over the fireplace and a library of books on the Polish underground in the living room?"

"Better than this empty penthouse you live in. It's nice, but I can't even tell it's you." I knew he was just pushing my buttons.

"There are cigarettes in the kitchen drawers and books on mathematical fallacies and paradoxes on the shelves. That's as much personality as I have." He laughed as he threw the last of the papers into the fire. The ash was gathering in piles underneath the logs, limiting the airflow inside the hearth. I sighed with relief to know we were done.

"Thanks. Can you put these suitcases back into the bedroom?" I asked. Emil nodded and disappeared with the luggage.

Just then, a soft knock came at the door. I motioned down the hallway for Emil to stay back while I greeted Kacper. Emil leaned his back against the wall of the hallway, around the corner and out of sight from the main entrance. I tossed him the loaded Beretta from the coffee table in the living room, smoothed my dress and my hair, and opened the door calmly.

"Come in," I welcomed Kacper inside, then promptly shut the door behind him. I locked the dead bolt, then turned around, leaning against the door and crossing my arms.

"I let myself in with the residents walking into the building. I brought coffee," Kacper said, setting two carryout cups on the kitchen counter.

"And I have breakfast," I responded, nodding to the hallway where Emil walked out, armed with the Beretta. "I hope you're hungry. Sit down."

Kacper immediately raised his hands in the air and backed away.

"Joanna?" Kacper asked feebly. The look in his eyes indicated he had never been held at gunpoint.

"Sit." I pointed to the wing-backed leather armchair next to the fireplace, whose glowing embers were still sitting hot at the bed of the hearth.

"Who the hell is this?"

"Don't worry about him. Look at me and answer my questions." I walked towards him, my arms still crossed. "You were wired last night. Why?"

"What are you talking about?"

"I patted you down. Don't play stupid, and don't make me strip search you right now."

Kacper looked exasperated, and I knew he was deciding between keeping silent and risking his life for whomever hired him.

"I'm not wired today, and I don't know anything," he finally said after a moment of hesitation.

"Who hired you?" I asked, walking closer. As the fearful look on his face confirmed my concern from the night before, my urge for a cigarette rose.

"I don't know."

"Don't make me ask again," I pressured him as Emil cocked the Beretta behind me. Kacper started breathing faster.

"They called me, told me what to do, then wired me the cash into my bank account."

"How much did you do it for?"

"20,000. Does it matter?"

"Just checking what your honor is worth," I said, pacing the room towards Emil. I sent him a glance, which he received, understanding I wanted his input. Emil walked to Kacper, who still had his hands raised, and dug into his coat pocket. Pulling out Kacper's phone, he unlocked it and scrolled through the recent calls he received. He dictated a phone number aloud to me, which I jotted down on a notepad in the kitchen. The number started with international code +48, a prefix we both recognized.

"We know you came for the papers," I accused Kacper based on his comment last night.

"What were you looking for?" Emil followed up with his own question.

"I don't even know. I was supposed to take any papers I could find with me or take pictures."

"Is he worth keeping?" Emil asked.

"I swear to God I won't talk. I only did it for the money. You know I'm a legitimate scholar here; I know you looked me up already. I'm here for the degree, then I go back to Poland. I swear!" Kacper defended himself before I even gave an opinion. My eyes met Emil's, who then swung the back of the handgun against Kacper's face. Kacper reeled over the side of the armchair holding his face, blood dripping from his nose onto my newly finished floors. Emil tossed the phone onto Kacper's lap in the chair.

"Don't contact them again."

"But they'll come looking for me. What do I do?"

"That's your problem. They'll finish you off, whoever they are," Emil explained.

"Get out of here," I said. "And leave the coffee."

"Joanna– " *Oh, please.*

"Now." I commanded. Kacper rose and slammed the door behind him as he left the condo.

Emil walked to the Chesterfield and collapsed into it, resting the gun on his knee and propping his head against the hand that rested on the arm of the couch.

"Well, that wasn't too helpful," I said, voicing what I knew we were both thinking.

"No. All we have is this phone number."

"And we're damn well not calling it, especially if it's Polish." I dropped onto the couch next to Emil and leaned forward, resting my elbows on my knees and my face in my hands.

"These people thought your grandfather was hiding something in his papers," mused Emil.

"And my grandfather knew he had secrets from the war…"

"Go on."

"Henryk must have known they would go through his things. He wouldn't have kept something in an obvious place."

"You're saying we burned all those documents for nothing?"

"I'm saying whoever hired Kacper was barking up the wrong tree."

I stood up again, Emil's comments prompting my imagination. I walked to the window and looked down, as I had the night before, watching a frantic Kacper scamper across the street. I smirked at his change in demeanor over the past 12 hours. Last night, he was smooth and sultry, playing with my risqué invitations. Now he was lost and alone, drained of any confidence he displayed before.

"If Dziadek knew we'd be destroying his personal belongings, he must have left something behind that wasn't so personal. It would have been on display, public."

"What about the military badges on his uniform at the wake?"

"Maybe… But those are six feet under. It's too late to recover them now."

I walked past the nearly vacant bookshelf leaning against the wall and gazed at the picture frames that still housed stock photos, the golden Cartier clock I received from Wujek as a graduation gift, and the limited pile of books that I stacked and organized, neurotically, by ISBN code.

Books.

"His war memoir." I lifted the top two books off the stack – Solzhenitsyn's *The Oak and the Calf* and Euclid's *Elements* – and pulled out my worn copy of *On the Call to Vilnius*.

"You think your grandfather memorialized war secrets in his internationally recognized best-selling book?" Emil laughed. I flipped through the first pages until I got to his dedication for me, scribbled in black ink with his own frail handwriting:

To my Joanna - my hope. You can do anything you set your mind to.

I ran my finger over his archaic words, realizing they were familiar.

"He wrote the same words in the letter I read aloud at the funeral yesterday. That's too much of a coincidence."

"Or it's an endearing phrase he used often with you. Let's not make this sensational, Joanna. This isn't the Cold War anymore. Anything that's worth knowing about 20ᵗʰ century Poland has already been found out, trust me."

"Tell that to the guy who was here surveilling my condo last night." I rose to retrieve my fur coat from the night before. I stuck my hand in the pocket and pulled out the folded envelope.

"Read this out loud." I handed Emil the paper, who gave me a look that screamed, *"Are you serious?"* He sighed, unfolded the letter, and started speaking the words on the page.

"It's vague," said Emil after he read the last line, shaking his head and handing the letter back to me.

"His parting words next to my name match the inscription on my copy of the book. Who else does he mention in the letter?"

"Just Radek, your dad, and Magda, your grandmother."

I read through the words again, expecting another clue to jump out at me, but Emil was right. It was vague. The same words could have been said by any deceased grandfather to any of his family.

"Your dad was like a mirror of his younger self," Emil tried again. "And your grandmother, his wife, was the key to his life…"

There it was.

"No, she wasn't."

"Sorry, what?"

"Babcia wasn't the key to my grandfather's life. She was his treasure. That's what he always called her, *mój skarb*, *skarbie*, the diminutives went on and on. I can still hear him saying that in my mind so clearly. She was his treasure his entire life because with her, he was the richest man in the world, he would say. Watch the video of the renewal of their vows at Trójcowo on their 50th wedding anniversary, he even says it into the priest's microphone."

"If she was his treasure– "

"Then why did he use the word *key*?"

"Her name is the key. Do you have another copy of the book?"

"Go to my bedroom, there's one in my nightstand drawer."

Emil left promptly, and the energy in the room skyrocketed as if we had discovered a gold mine. And maybe we had.

"Find every reference to Magda you can. Write it down and make sure you look at the context and the surrounding sentences. Start at the back, I'll start at the front," he said as he made his way down the hallway.

We sat next to each other for at least two hours, scanning every single page carefully. I had read the memoir at least a dozen times, so I knew which chapters referenced their marriage more explicitly than others, but I was sure to skim through every page in case there was something I was missing.

"I'm at page 200. You?" I asked.

"I've already passed it. Let's stop. Give me your notepad."

I gazed over his shoulder as he lay our papers next to each other on the coffee table:

21.	425.
22.	342.
47.	
54.	

After several minutes of staring at the numbers in front of us, Emil caved.

"You're the mathematician here; you figure this out. I'm starving." He stood up and walked to the fridge. I knew he would be disappointed.

"*Jezu Chryste*, don't you eat, woman?" He exclaimed slamming the door shut.

"Call for takeout. There's cash in the drawer next to the dishwasher." He groaned and then immediately called for the fastest delivery he could find in Gold Coast.

I tore the two pieces of notepad paper to separate each number and started rearranging them into different permutations on the table. My mind raced through every possibility of what they could represent.

There were either too many or too few digits to make up a phone number in either a European or American setting. I found the same issue with a bank account number. Any phone numbers or bank accounts that existed during the war wouldn't have been in use anymore, though. Both systems on both continents would have been refined since then.

I tried again with something less complicated – the alphabet. I then started tracing the numbers through the English alphabet, doubling back for the numbers higher than 26. I tried again with the Polish alphabet, which had more letters.

Nothing.

The food arrived, and Emil was happily snacking in the kitchen behind me while I continued working through the digits before me. I had other ideas for mathematical equations I could put together, but my grandfather was not a mathematician. He was just a simple miner, and he was practical. He would have coded this to something more accessible, something he knew.

"It has to be something he was familiar with, and something that wouldn't have changed from the time he fought in Poland during the war to at least the time he wrote his war memoir in the States. He never went back to Poland to ascertain any of these codes either, so it would be something that he knew would remain stagnant, even if he couldn't check on it."

"Coordinates," Emil said collectedly from the kitchen as he stuffed an egg roll into his mouth. I turned to him in disbelief to hear him speak again after he had satisfied his hunger, then turned back to the numbers splayed out in front of me on the coffee table. I brought my laptop from the kitchen to the living room and navigated to Google Maps to search the most common places my grandfather would have visited during the war.

"Amazing what a man can accomplish on a full stomach," I muttered as I typed in the city names mentioned in his war memoir.

"Buy me dinner and then you'll see just how helpful I can be," Emil said as he walked closer to me and stood behind the couch, looking over my shoulder. He had changed his cologne since the last time I saw him. Tom Ford was out, apparently, and Creed was in.

"He ran the Warsaw-Vilnius route most often," I said.

"Look for major cities along that diagonal."

I typed in Warsaw, then Łomża, then Augustów, then finally, Vilnius. As I monitored the changing of the coordinates along the geographic diagonal that Dziadek would have traveled, I realized that there was only one combination of the numbers in front of us that made sense.

"54. 21. 425. That's the north coordinate, it just needs a decimal between the two and the five. 22. 47. 342. That's the east, with its decimal."

"Search where that is," Emil said, coming around the corner of the couch. I hit enter as Google Maps panned out, then zoomed back in, focusing on a wooded plain with a single main road paved through it.

"It's the tripoint," I observed.

"Where Poland, Lithuania, and Russia meet. The Kaliningrad Oblast." Emil nodded, running his hand through his thick, dark hair. Both of our eyes remained on the screen.

"That's not a coincidence." I stood up after a few moments and paced the front of the room. I checked the clock on my bookshelf. It was only 1:00 in the afternoon. If we wanted to make it tonight, we had time.

"Go home and pack your bags," I said, turning back to Emil and the confetti of torn papers arranged on the coffee table. "We're going to Poland tonight."

5

On the way to the airport, Emil and I called Wujek on speakerphone to update him on our discovery that morning. I assumed he would be worried for our impulsive decision to book a same-day transatlantic flight together, but when he heard the whole story, he could not have been more elated. It was as if he were endeavoring on the same adventure with us. It was impossible to get him to stop rambling about the trip. When he got excited and his words seemed to work faster than his thoughts, he always defaulted to speaking in Polish.

"When you get to Warsaw and your cousin picks you up, make sure to stop by the Powązki Military Cemetery on your way to her condo– "

"Wujek, it's so far out of the way– "

"And place a wreath and two candles at the memorial monument of Łupaszka. Please do this for me. One candle is from me, one candle is from your grandfather. He was a great commander of our brigade, and he was murdered by the communists, you understand?"

"I do."

"And if you have the opportunity, please bring back a bottle of Żubrówka at the end of your trip. Don't be cheap, get me the big bottle. They don't sell that at any Polish stores around here– "

"Actually, they just started selling it in– "

"And bison grass is just a rare form of distilled liquor that one cannot replicate in this country. Hell, I should have gone with you. Why didn't you invite me?"

Emil and I stifled our laughter as we huddled towards the phone in the car, listening to the man whose energy levels were decades younger than his physical age.

"Next time, Dziadek," Emil responded to his grandfather.

"Fine. I phoned Agata's husband this afternoon, he's going to make the… arrangements you will need for your trip to the north. They have a car for you."

"Excellent. We'll call you in the morning when you're awake."

"Don't call too early, and don't make your calls too long. When you call long distance, you know, the rates are astronomical." I smiled, knowing he still understood landlines, but not Wifi-enabled audio calls.

"I'll cover any bills you receive, don't worry."

"And for God's sake, don't call the mobile phone, make sure you use the home phone! I don't want to deal with Horizon Wireless in these international situations you both force me into."

"Verizon," Emil said.

"Huh?"

"Never mind. We love you and will call you tomorrow."

"Have a safe flight. *Szerokiej drogi.*" Emil hung up and stashed his phone in the breast pocket of his topcoat. Both of us knew how to dress for these long flights, and neither of us could trade style for comfort. It should be functional, yes, but anything resembling polyester was out of the question. Our relatives in Poland were far less forgiving when judging by appearance, and the cousin picking us up from the airport was especially ruthless.

We passed through O'Hare TSA, had a martini at the bar near the gate, and then seated ourselves in first class. I was asleep before the plane took off on the overnight flight, then found myself receiving a warm towel and black coffee from the stewardess six hours later. Emil was already awake, reading some annotated stack of papers.

"Good morning," he greeted me as I transitioned my reclined chair into a seated position.

"Hi. You're working already?" I asked, gesturing to the manuscript in his hand and rubbing my eyes.

"It's for a book."

"Are you reviewing or writing?"

"Writing."

"What is it, your fifth publication? Give me that, let me see," I stole the papers from his hands and unrolled the manuscript to look at the cover page.

"It's a dissection of the Wołyń massacre and the stain it has left on postwar Polish-Jewish relations."

"Hasn't there been enough written about this already?" I flipped through the first few pages and skimmed the abstract.

"Yes, but not by an American."

"What's your take?"

"It was a horrific event, but it disproportionately skewed the perception of Polish anti-Semitism on a global stage."

"You're going to have a tough time finding a crowd to accept that thesis, especially in the States," I commented, sipping on my warm beverage. There was something about the first coffee on the flight from Chicago to Warsaw that transformed me. The journey over the ocean was so romantic and passionate, leaving behind the bustling country of capitalism, productivity, and work towards the ancient continent of leisure, art, and love.

"Then they can write their own book about it." Emil plucked the manuscript from my hands and returned to his reading.

We landed two hours later at Chopin International Airport. As we strolled out of the terminal, I saw my mother's niece, Agata, waiting for us with her husband, Marek.

"There they are!" She squealed from afar. Her energy had always been far beyond mine, even at my most enthusiastic, but it was always alluring. We exchanged hugs and handshakes and then loaded our luggage into their Fiat.

"We need to make a stop," I said once we were on the expressway. "Marek, can you roll down the window?"

"Where do you need to be already? You just got here," Agata asked as I lit my last Djarum Black. I hadn't restocked before we departed and would probably need to settle for Camels for the remainder of my time in Europe.

"Wujek wants us to go to Powązki." I took a drag of my cigarette, awaiting the onslaught of criticism towards my request.

"Are you serious? You're being pursued internationally by some unknown predator two days after your grandfather's funeral, and he wants you to honor his old commander abroad before you even have a chance to shower?"

"Just do it, Agata. The cemetery is in Żoliborz just past your condo, anyway."

"Fine, but you smell like death."

"That's not me, that's Emil." I took another puff, then added, "Besides, we're here on the business of the dead."

I bought a wreath and two candles from an elderly woman in the booth at the entrance of the cemetery with the leftover Polish currency from my last trip that I had scraped together at home.

The woman handed me the plastic bag with my purchase, and the four of us strolled down the dreary walkways of the national military cemetery.

It was the Arlington of Poland. I came here often with Dziadek and my parents when we traveled to Warsaw. Dziadek would walk me, a little girl, through the winding paths and past the impressive monuments marking the tombs of his deceased countrymen. It seemed anyone who my grandfather had known from his time in the war was buried here. His commander, two of his brothers, and my father's godfather were all lying beneath the hallowed ground we walked.

To supplement my grandfather's hatred of secularized American funeral customs, he also could not fathom why Americans held such a stigma against cemeteries. For them, it was representative of ghosts and spiritual unrest, while for Poles it was where their family and friends rested, and where every human would eventually lie. His favorite holiday, All Souls Day, honored that history, and Dziadek, like most Catholic Poles, adorned the graves of his family every year on the second of November. He did it as a young man in Poland for his deceased family members, and he continued the tradition in

America for his wife and son. In fact, that might have been why he declined a burial at Powązki, even though a plot of this highly coveted cemetery was offered to him by the Polish government later in his life. He wanted to be near my grandmother, his wife, his treasure.

As we neared Łupaszka's memorial, I started to feel the same respect for the dead bubble up in me at the cemetery that surrounded us. Though it was April, and we were months away from the next All Souls Day, there were still numerous people gathered at the cemetery, cleaning gravestones and praying. It wasn't a holiday; we were just there on a normal workday, a Monday afternoon.

I took out my Zippo lighter to light the two candles as Emil leaned the wreath against the commander's monument. Fresh bouquets of roses, prayer cards, and rosaries already decorated the same marker, telling us silently we weren't the only ones who remembered Łupaszka.

"Incredible that they haven't found his body yet," Marek said behind us. I heard the strike of a match, then turned to him for another cigarette. He offered me a menthol.

"You can't even call this a grave, not until they find him. Just a memorial site," Agata said, shaking her head.

"*Żołnierze wyklęci*, the Damned Soldiers. That's what our grandfathers were, too, before they escaped Poland. The war didn't end in 1945 for them. They still had the communists to defeat for a free country," Emil commented with a deep sigh. Marek nudged his arm to offer him a menthol and the matchbox, which Emil accepted. I hadn't remembered that he smoked, but when speaking of death, sometimes one must. He looked like he was tempting me while doing it, too.

"Imagine choosing whether to defend your country and risk your life or leave the country you love in order to live," I contemplated. "Impossible choices back then."

"Not many people think like that anymore. They do what's easy, what's lucrative," Agata took the box of cigarettes from Emil and was the last of us four to light herself one.

"Instead of what's right," I finished her sentence while she took a drag. She nodded and exhaled, the smoke rising across her face and past her dramatic sunglasses.

After a few more moments at the monument, we dropped our cigarette butts one by one and left in silence. Whether others prayed silently, I wasn't sure. My mind was on the trip we'd be taking the next day.

6

"Come with me after you've freshened up. I'll show you the spread, and then we'll go out to dinner," Marek said to us after we came through the door of their condo. The smell from the vase of springtime lilacs, which had not yet bloomed in Chicago, came over us before we even set our luggage on the ground. Agata and Marek lived in a quiet quarter called Wola, west of the Warsaw city center, and had two guest bedrooms to host us that night. I was relieved to know they were in town that week. Staying in the home of a hospitable family far outweighed the luxuries of any hotel in this country.

Agata finally took off her sunglasses in order to see more clearly inside her refrigerator. She pulled out a platter of smoked meats and cheeses, a bowl of Olivier salad, and a fresh loaf of sliced rye bread. Emil and I each rolled our luggage into our respective bedrooms but came out to the living room before we unpacked to help ourselves to the food being offered.

"Drinks are in order, I presume?" Agata asked, setting out bottles of wine on the table next to the hors d'oeuvres.

"Emil, we have Okocim and Tatra in the fridge, if you're up for a beer," Marek added.

"Tatra," Emil responded, loading a small plate with food.

"You two don't want to shower first?" Agata asked. "Never mind. You're starving, I'm sure." We had already begun devouring the sandwiches we each made from the bread, meat, and cheese. As soon as I swallowed my last bite, I stood up.

"I'll have the wine," I said. Marek poured a glass of merlot and took two bottles of Tatra from the fridge, handing one to Emil.

"Leave some room for dinner," Agata laughed.

"Are you implying Warsaw finally got its first Michelin star restaurant after the fall of communism?" I asked, smiling back. My cousin rolled her eyes.

"I will have you know that we have not one, but at least *10* Michelin star restaurants already. But that's not where we're going. Go with Marek, he'll show you what he has arranged."

Emil and I followed Marek to their bedroom, where an array of over a dozen guns, ranging from modern assault rifles to communist era revolvers, awaited us on the bed.

"Holy shit," Emil said.

"Feels like you're in summer self-defense camp in Zakopane with us again, huh?" Asked Marek.

"I haven't seen this many arms since then," I added in shock. I was impressed.

"What did you say you did for a living again?" Emil asked, running his hands over the dark, matte metal bodies of the guns.

"I used to be with counterintelligence at the *Służba Kontrwywiadu Wojskowego*, but now I just hold an office job with the Ministry of Transportation," Marek answered. "When you've spent as many years in the field as I have, you realize that getting to wear a gun and badge every day isn't as sexy as you thought it was when you were younger."

"Still, when you know some people who know some people, you can get a lot in Poland,"

Agata said from behind us. Her arms were crossed as she leaned against the doorframe to the bedroom. "Even in the Ministry of Transportation."

"So, what do you think this could be?" I asked. Marek sighed in response to my heavy question.

"Wujek called me before he went to bed last night and explained what you told him. We would get tips on cases like this sometimes. Very James Bond, you know: secret villain is after some unknown secret related to some past event or relationship, and now there's this whole international chase." He sat down on the edge of the bed and continued.

"This Kacper guy pursued you immediately after your grandfather's death, meaning there was a reason the pursuer couldn't act before. Perhaps you were easier to get to than your grandfather was. I don't think a 30-year-old male could seduce a 96-year-old man, but I've been wrong before. The subject they are seeking is something you are unaware of, but they were under the impression that there was information about that subject in the papers you had at your place.

"Your grandfather was aware that these people would come after his possessions following his death, so instead of hiding something physically within his belongings, he employed this cryptography, which you decoded using his postmortem letter as the key, revealing the coordinates of Poland's northern tripoint where Russia, Lithuania, and Poland meet. His knowledge of that area would have been extensive during the war, since he fought with Wachlarz and was assigned to defend Vilnius, which is about a five-hour drive from Warsaw.

"Now you have this phone number with a Polish international code. That doesn't necessarily mean that those who are pursuing you are Polish or that they are even located in Poland, but they certainly have some kind of connection within the country because they acquired the phone here. Am I missing anything?"

We shook our heads, grateful that someone else understood the situation and for the recap of the events of the past 48 hours.

"Good. What year did your grandfather leave Poland?" Marek asked, looking at me.

"1946."

"One year after the end of the war. Those coordinates were no coincidence, since the national borders of these three countries would have been established by that time. I think there is something hidden there that these people want to make sure someone else doesn't find."

"So why come after his things after he's already dead? When he was alive, he could have told anyone in the world, he could have told Wujek, he could have told me," I thought out loud, my eyes scanning the weapons again.

"My grandfather said that your Dziadek wanted to protect you, right?" Emil asked.

"Well, it's certainly not helping me now that he's gone. But you're right. He probably kept this from others because he was trying to protect them," I said.

"Or because he was sworn to secrecy by someone," Marek suggested.

"Perhaps there are more clues in the book?" I suggested.

"Doubtful. Typically, when we see a paper trail throughout a chase like this, a person wouldn't use the same key twice. It would be too obvious. Forget the memoir. Tomorrow, your starting place is whatever lies at those coordinates."

"Have either of you ever been up there?" Emil asked.

"The tripoint? No. There's nothing up there, probably just a small drive-through town and a lot of border security," Agata answered, still in the doorway.

"I'm arming you because we have to assume these people can move and act quickly. Kacper certainly will not be calling them to say he broke upon the slightest pressure and, if they come for him and later appear at your condo in Chicago, they'll know you've gone to Poland already. Assume they're waiting for you."

I felt a rush of adrenaline, a burst of energy that made me want to leave for the north that very same night. I wouldn't get a good night's sleep without a relaxant. I needed a drink and another cigarette.

"Let's go to dinner," I said, changing the subject. There was no use in ruminating over the possibilities that lie ahead for tomorrow without knowing what, or who, awaited us at the tripoint.

7

The next morning, I was awake at 7:00, my body still adjusting to the time change, but early enough to resume my routine of listening to the Polish news channel while making myself espresso in Agata's kitchen. Within the hour, Emil and I were washed, dressed, and packed into my cousin's Alfa Romeo, whose smell, cleanliness, and low mileage indicated its recent purchase.

The sun was beginning to rise over quiet Warsaw as we rolled out of the underground garage of Agata and Marek's condo building into the empty street. Emil drove the stick shift as I gazed out the window at the city whose people, like us, were just starting their day. Cigarette-smoking, hungover men were cranking up the graffiti-marked aluminum rollers that covered the barred windows of their newspaper kiosks. Older women with headscarves wrapped around their faces and tied under their chins walked in pairs to the nearest church for daily Mass. Children were leaving their urban homes to wait at their bus stops for another day at school. Stray dogs sniffed through the garbage piles in the alleys between concrete apartment buildings. The smell of fresh bread rose with the steam coming from bakeries. Buckets of freshly cut roses and tulips appeared on the sidewalks, inviting customers inside their flower shops.

These scenes in Warsaw were as grey and industrial as I had always remembered them to be, but every year I visited the city, I noticed more and more of the funding from the European Union reflected in the infrastructure. This time, I saw the clunky, decrepit trams had been replaced by bright, sleek, red and yellow ones that even displayed their destination on a digital screen in the front window. The old paper signs that the railway conductors posted with each route had finally been ousted.

Once we entered the expressway and left the Warsaw city limits, Emil finally started speaking. Growing up with him, I knew he needed an hour or two to acclimate to the day after waking up before he could speak amiably.

The silence didn't bother me; it just gave me more time to enjoy the morning imagining the tripoint.

"After all that time you spent at the Sorbonne, surrounded by the most attractive and intelligent European men, you still couldn't find someone who met your standards?"

"Such a brash question for such an early morning of an eventful day," I said playfully. I picked a small feather off my parka, as if the pointed inquiry didn't affect me. "I suppose no one quite fit the mold."

"You have a mold?" Emil asked. I turned the radio on and left the preset local jazz station instead of switching the genre of music. I didn't particularly like jazz; I just wanted to avoid a potential reprimand from Agata for changing the settings of her new car.

"Everyone has a mold. Yours is young and sexy, apparently, with no affinity for high literature," I joked. Perhaps it was too early for below-the-belt insinuations like that.

"Shakespeare best summarized my partners."

"How?"

"Highly fed and lowly taught," Emil responded, keeping his eyes on the road. I looked at him, relieved to know he was in a good mood for the long drive ahead, and laughed at the comment.

"Ugh, please don't use the word partner," I requested. "It makes it sound like you don't ever want to– "

"Get married?"

"Yes."

"What's so great about commitment?"

"I don't know, why don't we ask our grandparents who were all able to sustain over 60 years of marriage?" I looked out the window again, turning my back on Emil and the conversation that I knew would highlight our differences yet again. The mood in the car changed quickly, as if someone had flipped a switch. I knew he sensed my distance. Emil jumped around from woman to woman, but he was not the reason why those relationships ever ended. He had his choice, always, and had never had his heart broken. He knew how to read women, and his intuition with them was what made him so approachable and attractive.

"Why do you think you and I never tried to work anything out?" Emil asked after a short silence.

"Oh God, don't start this conversation." I smoothed my hands over my pants, visibly flustered.

"We've never talked about it, and I've always wondered. You're a bold woman, why did you never approach me?"

"I'll tell you what I think, but you have to tell me your opinion first," I turned the question around on him and revolved my body to face him again, crossing my arms over my chest. I felt my heart pounding through my shirt against the watch on my wrist that pressed into my rib cage. At the very least, the discussion was keeping my mind off our eventual arrival at the tripoint.

"Fine," he said, his eyes still on the road. "You always seemed so independent. I didn't feel I could get close to you, even though we spent our entire childhood together. Even through our summers in Poland when we seemed to spend every waking minute together at the self-defense camp, whether it was at the shooting range or at the bonfires at night, you were always so distant. You thought you were better than anyone else, and you were. You were smarter, more ambitious, more beautiful."

My eyes darted from Emil to the road. I did not have a defense prepared. I sat with the truth he laid out in front of me and admitted to myself that it was the same reason I hadn't secured a serious relationship throughout my entire adult life. I had built a wall to protect myself, and it accomplished what I needed, whether I liked the end result or not: it kept others out.

"Your turn," said Emil, flashing a smile in my direction. I rolled my eyes, succumbing to what I had agreed to do.

"You were too arrogant with women."

"That's all I get?" Emil asked, still grinning. He knew what I was saying was true. I sighed with exasperation, knowing I owed him a better explanation.

"Emil, you always had a girlfriend, from the time we were in high school. I don't blame them. You are brilliant and motivated and so goddamn good looking. You are irresistible, I get it. But you never had a break."

I paused, and he glanced my way. His smile was gone, but it was replaced by a satisfied look of understanding and clarity. Our eyes met for a brief second before his returned to the road.

"There was never any room for me," I concluded.

"I think, in a way, we never made room for each other. Even though it would have seemed to the rest of the world like the most natural opportunity for us to take," Emil mused, wrapping up my thoughts in the most perfect way. I paused again before offering my suggestion.

"We can try on this trip, Emil. I know it sounds stupid, since we're halfway across the world chasing God-knows-whom."

"Bonnie and Clyde, remember?" Emil resurrected the reference I thought had been dead to him since our last summer camp.

"Sounds familiar."

We continued the drive through the springtime prairies and forests, stopping once for gas. I couldn't stop thinking about Emil's words and wondered how long he had felt this way about me. If I had had any kind of experience in a serious relationship, I probably would have taken advantage of the time alone in the car to ask my questions, but the silence felt equally as compelling, knowing we had finally cleared the air between us. The drive, which normally would have seemed dull, now appeared to be colorful and dramatic. And anytime Emil's eyes met mine, even in the silence, he emoted more than his words could describe.

8

The further north we drove, the more Poland seemed to be stuck in winter rather than entering spring. A thin layer of snow still covered the ground, and the sky was overcast. I was fortunate to have remembered my parka, a tip from Helena as we quickly packed prior to the flight. I ditched the Canada Goose to opt for something less ostentatious. The less I looked like I had just landed from America, the better.

Emil finally announced we were nearing our destination, 54°21'42.5"N 22°47'34.2"E. When Marek realized Agata's Alfa Romeo was not able to map to an exact latitude and longitude, he gave us his spare phone, which was programmed with a secure GPS system he could still connect to, from his prior position with the military. The tripoint area was a generic term and could have led us to any number of villages near the Russian/Lithuanian border, so we were adamant about driving to the exact coordinates we found in the memoir.

We approached a road that crossed expressway DW651 and paused at the first landmarks we had seen in several kilometers. Emil slowed to a halt at the stop sign and remained there for several seconds before driving on.

"What do you think?" He asked as we both looked out the window at our surroundings. I accounted for one gas station, one restaurant, one church, and an empty parking lot, each situated on its own corner of the intersection.

"I say we park and take a walk. I should stretch my legs."

Emil turned into the empty parking lot as I opened the glove compartment and took out the two Walther PPQs, handing one to Emil below the dashboard in case anyone was near the car. We each checked that our guns were loaded and stuffed them into our belts behind our backs, concealing them underneath our parkas.

We stepped out of the car. The air was as cool and fresh as I imagined it would have been, away from any major city and surrounded by countless hectares of pastures and forests. We walked off to the side of DW651, passing signs that said *Trójstyk Granic*, signaling the tripoint of borders to visitors, and informational boards in various languages that listed the documentation required to enter Russia or Lithuania.

"You think we'll just stumble upon it? Or know it when we see it?" I asked after several minutes of walking east along the expressway. Only one car passed us during our entire walk. I could hear the cows mooing ahead at the next pasture.

"I wish it were that easy. We came all this way and don't even know what we're looking for. How far until we leave the confines of coordinates we drove to?"

"Not far," I answered. "Each degree of latitude or longitude is only 70 miles or so apart from the next. If we're trying to locate the exact minute and second of the coordinate, we shouldn't stray too far from where we stopped."

I lit a cigarette and we turned around, heading back to the intersection where we parked. There was no traffic in the area, and the car seemed undisturbed, so we crossed to the other side of DW651 and decided to enter the restaurant.

The small eatery was quaint and nearly empty. The sound of the faint radio played from a speaker at the cash register. An old woman, close to Wujek's age, was steeping her tea bag in hot water in a dark corner, staring into her cup. A young waiter was washing dishes at the coffee bar. Two middle aged men sat at the bar across from him, hunched over what looked like shots of vodka.

Emil and I lowered ourselves into the seats of the table nearest to the door. The waiter approached us and asked for our drink order. We each switched to our fluent Polish without trace of a foreign accent.

"I'll have a beer. Żywiec. You, *kochanie*?" Emil asked across the table. The affectionate name made my heartbeat speed up, but I caught on to his act immediately and played along for the waiter.

"I'll do a glass of wine. It's already noon. Why not? Let's celebrate!" I reached across the table with my left hand and took his hand. He leaned forward, faking some over-the-top infatuation. Under the table, I finagled the diamond ring I wore on my middle finger over to my ring finger. I was lucky I had it on the same hand that engaged women wore their rings in this country, and not on my left hand.

"Anniversary trip?" The waiter asked, delightfully jotting down our orders on his notepad.

"We just got engaged!" I exclaimed, holding up my right hand with the newly placed diamond ring.

"Congratulations! Drinks, then, are on the house. I'll be back with those right away. In the meantime, please take a look at our menu. Our special today is the gołąbki in mushroom sauce." He set the paper menus in front of us and walked back to the coffee bar.

I released Emil's hand, still forcing a smile, and pretending like this was the happiest day of my life. In a sense, after the conversation we had in the car, it was. Part of my giddiness was artificial, though, as I realized we could be sitting in the belly of the beast. I gazed at the menu with a blank stare as I set up in my head the arrangement of the café, including everyone's position and distance from me. Emil, I knew, was doing the same from his angle.

I hadn't chosen a meal for lunch, so I finally took the time to read the menu, whose header spelled out *Café Gadam*, the second word meaning "I'm chatting." I smirked at the irony of the name of the restaurant, which seemed to boast few and rather unsocial customers that afternoon.

The waiter returned with our drinks, and we placed our orders.

"I'll have the blueberry pierogi," I said, sliding the menu across the table towards the waiter.

"And I'll have the lunch special," Emil responded. As he brought his beer closer to him, he revealed the header of his menu lying upside down from me. The name of the restaurant, as I looked at it from a different perspective, caught my eye.

"Shall I take your menus?" The waiter asked.

"You can leave one," I said before Emil could open his mouth, smiling at the young man. I placed my hand on Emil's menu, reinforcing my request. The waiter bowed slightly and disappeared into the kitchen.

"Emil," I whispered calmly as he took a sip of his beer. "The name of the café."

"Café Gadam?" He asked, setting his glass down. I watched the look on his face change as the same realization hit him. He scanned his menu to assess the letters again. His wide eyes confirmed what I was thinking: it was an anagram.

I rearranged the letters of the second word of the restaurant name in my head again: *Magda*.

I gave him a sharp, worried look, demanding him to make the call on our next move.

"We're here. It's here. This is the place," I started whispering frantically.

"Stay calm," he said. Emil leaned back in his seat with his beer, taking another sip. He seemed much more comfortable investigating potential enemy territory than I was. I mirrored him, leaning back, and took another sip of my wine. We were both facing the main area of the restaurant now, our backs to the entrance, memorizing as much of the layout of Café Gadam as possible. I looked at the floor-to-ceiling shelves of books, flowers, and other village-themed memorabilia. I gazed at the beams that crossed the ceiling and any possible signs or engravings above my head.

Then I analyzed the worn wooden floor and noticed a circular rug in between tables towards the back corner of the seating area. The rug was discrete, but its placement was peculiar. It wasn't underneath a single table, and it wasn't in a central or attractive location on the floor. It was serving a purpose where it lay. The rug was covering something.

"Call the number," I said. Emil pulled out his phone and scrolled to the +48 number he had saved to his phone from Sunday's encounter with Kacper. He selected it, then set his phone on the table quietly. Moments later, a phone from across the room began ringing. Without moving my head, I shifted my eyes to the coffee bar and watched as one of the men sitting behind his shot of vodka answered the call coming through.

"It might be Kacper..." I heard him whisper. "Hello?"

As soon as we saw the man had answered Emil's call, we stood up promptly and headed towards the door of the restaurant, but it was too late to leave without being noticed. Just then, four men in dark clothing appeared from the kitchen behind the coffee bar, armed with handguns, walking towards us. Emil and I sprinted out of the restaurant towards the parked car. The men were tall and bulky, but slow. They started shooting their guns. The bullets ricocheted off the ground and pierced the tall trees that stood past the parking lot in front of us.

"Stop!" They yelled across the road. Emil and I used the car to take cover, then unlocked the door and climbed in from the passenger side. Emil jumped over the main console, agilely started the car, and sped out off the parking lot towards the nearest paved road, taking us south.

"Shit," he said as we drove down the expressway, the men from Café Gadam disappearing into the horizon behind us. I turned to look at him and saw he was holding his right shoulder. A bullet had penetrated his parka, and blood stained his camel-colored wool sweater.

"Oh God. I'm calling Marek. Can you drive?" I asked, pulling out my phone.

"I'll be fine. Just ask him where we should go."

Marek provided an address in the next major city, Suwałki, and said he was leaving immediately and would meet us there in a few hours. I didn't provide any details, but he said he knew that if others were shooting at us at the tripoint, then we had found the right place.

9

Half an hour south of the tripoint, we arrived at the address, which led us to a small farm home. I got out of the car first and knocked on the door. A woman, about the age my parents would have been if they were alive, opened the door.

"Marek sent us," I said immediately.

"He called me. Where is Emil?" The woman asked.

"In the car," I gestured to the Alfa Romeo. "There's blood."

The woman disappeared into her house and returned seconds later with a white cloth. She gently pushed me aside and walked past me to the car, opening the driver's door and helping Emil to his feet and into the rickety house. I locked the car and followed them into the house, closing the door behind me.

The house was humble but comfortable and had quite obviously been passed down in the family through generations. The outdated furniture and portraits hanging on the wall all indicated that this woman had inherited the house and probably hadn't made many changes since her original acquisition.

"No one followed you?" The woman asked as she led Emil into the kitchen, seating him in a chair.

"Not that I saw," I said, feeling stupid for not even glancing once over my shoulder as we drove from the tripoint.

"No," Emil confirmed, grimacing over the pain.

"My name is Janina. I am a hospital nurse. I'm going to have to check your shoulder for shrapnel."

Janina stripped Emil from the waist up, revealing his sculpted body, and positioned him in a way where she could see the bullet hole best. She had metal forceps, disinfectant, and gauze on the kitchen table next to Emil, ready for the operation. Janina started, and spoke as she worked, as if she were knitting a sweater and not salvaging his shoulder.

"My mother fought in Wachlarz, too," she explained. The common origin of our families immediately gave me some peace of mind. "That's why we live so close to the Lithuanian border up here. Your grandfathers fought for Vilnius, no?"

"Yes," I answered. I pulled out the chair next to Emil and took his hand. He squeezed it, acknowledging my solidarity next to him. I smiled softly as he looked up at me.

"And you are Agata's cousin? Agata is your mother's niece?"

"Yes, my grandfather was Henryk Sosna."

"Did he fight in Wachlarz? I don't know the name."

"He did. Our predecessors all fought for the same organization and somehow their descendants are still connected, as fate would have it," I said.

"Not fate. God," Janina remained focused on her operation. "It happens in the military. I suppose we just don't know how to give up our duty to our country, even generations later. The apples don't fall far from the tree. Or maybe they can't." She continued to remove bits of the bullet. Every piece she pulled out, she dropped into a metal dish with a *clink*.

Janina tediously worked through Emil's shoulder until every bit of visible shrapnel was removed. She then bandaged him and put his arm in a makeshift sling.

"You're lucky it hit you so high. It only grazed your trapezius, didn't touch your scapula. There wasn't much to remove, really. You will heal quickly."

"Let's keep the shrapnel," Emil said.

"Do want you want," Janina responded, and handed him a plastic, sealable bag from a kitchen drawer.

After cleaning her medical utensils, Janina proceeded to the kitchen and transformed from field nurse to top chef. Within the hour, hunter's stew and fresh bread appeared on platters in front of us on the dining table. Emil and I dove into the familiar meal, tearing the bread into shreds and dipping it in the juices flowing from the hot medley of cabbage, mushrooms, and pork shoulder.

As we soaked up the last of the stew with our bread, she set a bottle of vodka and shot glasses on the table. The liquor was presumably homemade, judging by the lack of labeling on the bottle.

"I should have offered this before I took the bullet pieces out of your shoulder, but it seems like you two need the drink," Janina said, wiping her hands on her apron and returning to the sink to finish the dishes.

Suddenly, a knock came at the door. I looked at my watch and then at Emil across the table, knowing it was too early for Marek to have driven all the way from Warsaw. Emil rose from his seat and I followed his lead, pulling the gun out from my belt. Janina walked to the front door, opened it quietly, and stepped back to allow an older woman with a small, hunched over frame into the house. As soon as the woman turned the corner into the kitchen, my stomach dropped.

It was the same woman who we saw steeping tea in the corner of Café Gadam.

Confused at the coincidence, Emil and I both gripped our pistols harder, but the woman, glancing our way, raised one hand in midair and calmed us.

"At ease," she said wearily. The woman shuffled across the worn floor of the kitchen, as she had surely done her entire life in this house, with her cane and lowered herself into the seat I had just vacated. Emil and I looked at each other, then lowered our guns and pushed them back into our belts.

"May I ask what is going on?" I finally spoke once the woman was settled in her chair. She had taken off her headscarf, revealing the deep wrinkles in her skin. She was running her hands over her thick, white hair, assembled into a bun at the nape of her neck. She was old, perhaps the same age as my grandfather, but she moved with a hidden youth inside her. She didn't fumble with her cane or headscarf and her eyes looked around sharply, fully aware of her surroundings.

"They were at Café Gadam just now," the woman said, looking up at Janina, whose hands were on her hips.

"Marek called and sent them after they left," Janina said. "He didn't give me the details. I had no idea you were all at the same place."

"Did you follow us?" Asked Emil.

"I didn't need to. I live here," she responded. "This is my daughter, Janina."

"This is Emil Łowicki. I'm Joanna Sosna."

"Zygmunt's grandson?" The woman clarified. Emil nodded. "But Sosna... I don't know the name. You grandfather was in Wachlarz, too?"

"Yes," I confirmed. "And what is your name?"

She looked up at me with her grey-blue eyes.

"Magda."

Had the Vilnius segment of Wachlarz been thousands, or even hundreds, of members large, I would have brushed off the common Polish name as a coincidence. But with the significance, the key, that this name had become, I made the comment that I hoped would tie up some loose ends of our story.

"My grandmother's name was Magda."

My observation seemed to make an impression on this new Magda that I had just met. Her eyes widened and she gestured for us to sit at the table with her.

"At the end of the war, the boys needed to get out of Poland. They were hunted, called the Damned Soldiers, and if they stayed in their country that they had just fought six years to protect, they would be arrested and killed by the communists, usually in secret. Some of them stayed, but many of them had to leave if they wanted to live.

"My friend had been married in Warsaw, spent the war separated from his new wife, but then reconnected with her in Warsaw after the war. If they wanted to live, though, they had to escape from Poland. Fearing they would be found by the communists who infiltrated the country starting in 1945, they needed alternative documents. I worked with Wachlarz, but I was just a field nurse for the underground, so I wasn't in much danger. I gave up my passport to the woman."

"That woman was my grandmother," I said. "Everything you just told us was true, exactly how my grandfather told it to me when he was alive. And what about the man?"

"He had a double identity as part of Wachlarz throughout the war, so he disposed of his real identification and traveled on his pseudonym, I presume. We knew him as Radek Lasecki. And, of course, now that you tell me that Radek and Mariola were your grandparents, I see the resemblance in you, Joanna."

"Radek. Your father's name," Emil mentioned.

"'You were like a mirror of my younger self,'" I whispered to myself, recalling the words Dziadek used to describe my father in the letter I read aloud at the funeral.

"And then he changed it to Sosna," Magda continued out loud. Her eyes wandered from us to the table. She reached for the bottle of vodka, unscrewed the cap, and poured four shots clockwise.

"That gives a little more meaning to the name Magda, but it doesn't explain why you were at Café Gadam," Emil said, taking a shot glass into his hand.

"Those men shot at us. Who were they?" I asked. Magda looked at us, then at her daughter. Janina slid her shot glass towards her and motioned for her mother to continue speaking.

"You might as well tell them. If the guards were shooting at them, then Joanna and Emil have our common enemy. It's high time someone knows, Mama."

"Fine. I've lived a long enough life. *Na zdrowie*," Magda said, raising her glass. We joined her in the motion and took our shot along with her.

"Tell us. Maybe we can help each other," I said, setting my empty glass down.

"I'm sure we will. You'll have to bear with me," Magda started. "This story may seem improbable to you, but my daughter can confirm that what I am saying is true."

I nodded and leaned back in my chair. I reached into the pocket of my parka and, considering the rural farm home that was hosting us, I asked if I could smoke inside. Janina pulled down the window nearest me, then gestured for her mother to continue as she set a crystal ash tray in front of me.

"At the end of the war, before your grandfather made his last trip to Warsaw and then left the country, he was involved in... a project," Magda started pouring the next round of shots. "At that point, it was hard to know whom we could trust, so factions of the underground started operating on their own missions, doing their best to save Poland independently, without guidance from the government in exile in London. Your grandfather took a small platoon of men from Wachlarz to create an access point between three nations in the newly established borders of Europe. They were to dig a tunnel, two kilometers long, that would unite Poland, Lithuania, and the Kaliningrad Oblast of Russia beneath the earth. The tunnel was a V shape, with the point of the V originating in Poland." Magda traced a V on the table with her finger, demonstrating the route as she spoke.

"You're telling me that there is a 60-year-old man-made underground tunnel that bypasses the border controls of three countries?" Emil regurgitated incredulously.

"I told you, it sounds improbable, but it's true."

"Why?" I asked. "Why would Poles want to get into the Soviet Union?"

"Surveillance. Information. The Damned Soldiers, the same ones who fought in the Polish underground during the war, knew that the war raged on between Poland, who wanted to be free, and the communist influence from the Soviet Union. Just like the Soviets had spies in Poland, the Poles had spies in the Soviet Union. But it was impossible to cross borders in broad daylight, especially if the soldiers' names were on a hit list. They couldn't use sea or air to get into the Soviet Union, either. The clandestine tunnel seemed like a good approach.

"But it wasn't used for long by the Poles. In 1946, right after the tunnel had been completed, the Soviets discovered the openings in the Lithuania forest. It was catastrophic for the Poles. The 20 of them spent over a year digging, only to hand over the tunnel on a silver platter to the very people who were hunting them.

"The Soviets' discovery of the passage was fatal for almost everyone. There was a mass execution carried out on the spot as soon as they found that Polish soldiers were in the Lithuanian leg of the tunnel. They killed everyone who was digging, except for two people."

Magda lifted her refilled glass, and we all took our second shot of vodka in tandem. I was grateful Janina left the bottle on the table. The story would have been much less believable without it.

"You can probably guess who the two survivors were," Magda said.

"Our grandfathers?" I asked.

"My grandfather separated from yours at the end of the war. They wrote letters, we even have them at home. So, it must have been Henryk, I mean, Radek, and..." Emil and I looked across the table.

"That's right. Radek and I were the only ones they allowed to live." Tears welled in Magda's eyes in the same way my grandfather's eyes did when he told his rare emotional stories.

"*Jezu Chryste...*" I said, burying my face in my hands, my cigarette dangling between my forefinger and middle finger in my right hand. I was absorbing everything at that moment – Magda's connection with my grandmother, my grandfather's survival, this supposed tunnel, and its coverup to this day. I couldn't tell if I needed more vodka or more sleep to understand it all.

"Why didn't you tell anyone about it? How is this tunnel still standing?" Emil asked.

"We were each blackmailed into secrecy. I remember the exact words they said to us. 'We are your occupiers now, and we will hunt you down to the ends of the earth if you ever speak word of this tunnel to anyone. We will kill your wives and husbands and children and grandchildren, no matter how much family you have, no matter when you speak of this tunnel again.'

"Radek was already married at that time, and I had parents and siblings to protect. We were young and scared. We had just survived six years of horrific war. We'd do anything to survive at that point. And they let us go because we bribed them with…" Magda looked into her lap. Her sharp eyes averted from our faces in shame. "With artillery and money that we stole from the underground."

"And you lived, Mama," Janina said softly, placing her hand on her mother's lap. Her tone made it clear that she had to provide this consolation to her mother's guilty conscience often. It sounded to me like a repeated reminder, a reminder that was crafted to assuage Magda's deep, old wounds of the past.

"Only because we were cowards," said Magda. "Not heroes. The heroes' bodies were dragged from the tunnel and thrown into the Lithuanian woods, one by one, without even a proper burial. I had to carry them with Radek myself."

"The war was a difficult time, Magda. No one blames you for making that choice. And here we are, decades later, still talking about the same tunnel. Maybe we can…" I searched for the right, delicate words. "Atone for the past. Together."

"In sacrificing the resources of my nation, I saved my family."

"So," I said, putting out my cigarette. "Only my grandfather and you knew about this tunnel? Just two people?"

"Three," said Janina. "My mother told me because I am the only person she has on this earth. I never knew my father and I have no siblings. And I've never told a soul."

"Magda, what were you doing at Café Gadam today?" Emil raised the same question I had on my mind since she entered the house.

"You don't think the Soviets took a tunnel like that and sat idle with it, do you?" Janina responded on behalf of her mother.

"Oh my God. They're still using it?" I asked, desperately pulling out my cigarettes again. Polish history had always been a thing of the distant past for Emil and me. It was something we listened to, read about, and studied, but now it was suddenly creeping into my life. My grandfather's legacy was meeting my own, and it was suffocating.

Magda and Janina looked more abashed now, hesitating to answer the question.

"And you're helping them?" Emil questioned further. They looked at each other. Janina folded her hands in her lap and Magda looked down again.

"It's still part of the blackmail, my children," Magda whispered. Tears fell from her eyes out of embarrassment. "They use me to transport things, and people..."

"You've been their mule since the end of the war? It's been over 60 years. But it makes sense. Instead of recruiting younger mules and making this known to more people, they're using the same person who knew all along, until the end of her days," I said out loud.

I stood up to pace the kitchen, uncomfortable with their silence. My entire life I had been taught honor and duty to country, but this was perhaps the first time I was faced with the challenges that came with it. Magda was needing to choose the life of her daughter over the integrity of her nation. It was an impossible choice, and one she had lived with for too long.

"Will you help us?" Magda asked me. Her plea, for the first time that afternoon, sounded vulnerable.

I took a long drag of my cigarette and looked at Emil, who was still staring at the women at the table.

"For your sake, and my grandfather's."

10

We spoke about Wachlarz and Magda's memories of the war, most of which were already written into *On the Call to Vilnius*, but Emil and I listened patiently to her, understanding that she probably had few visitors with whom she could share her stories. Two hours later, we heard the door of a car slam outside Magda and Janina's farm home. Emil and I straightened up in our seats as Janina went to the door to open it for Marek. He walked in abruptly without a greeting to first examine Emil.

"It grazed the top of his shoulder. The bullet went straight through without touching any bone, in and out. It was a clean shot, just some shrapnel left behind. He'll be fine," Janina explained, her arms crossed over her chest.

"Good. Now tell me what the hell happened at the tripoint," Marek said, sitting down. He unwrapped the scarf from around his neck and unzipped his coat. Janina set a clean shot glass down in front of him and slid the ash tray from my side of the table to the center. We recounted in detail the short encounter at Café Gadam, then paused to allow Magda and Janina explain the location of the small restaurant and what it was hiding.

"You are saying that there is an entrance to a two-kilometer tunnel that connects the three countries at the tripoint located directly beneath a derelict restaurant, Sosna coordinated the digging of this tunnel, and Magda has been manning it for the past 60 years?" Marek finally clarified once everyone had told their perspective of the story from that afternoon. He was leaning forward in disbelief, his coat now hanging on the chairback behind him, and gesturing with a half-smoked cigarette between his thumb and forefinger.

No one denied his clarification. After some more silence, Marek leaned back in his seat and took his shot, alone.

"Okay," he started, setting his glass back down and taking a long drag of his cigarette. "Here is what I know. After the collapse of the Soviet Union, the KGB was officially dissolved.

Following its dissolution, a radical faction of the organization, including those closest to the Kremlin, and some of them in very high positions of power in 1991, reformed into a small, quasi-terrorist political cooperative. These were people who felt the Soviet Union and its influence could not be impeded by its formal disintegration, and so they took matters into their own hands and operated off the grid.

"In the two decades since the Soviet Union's collapse, the organization has changed form many times and now resembles less of a governmental agency with a political agenda and more of a mafia with a profit motive, only with strong ties to the Russian government. We've traced hundreds of cases of criminal activity in Poland back to this group. You name it – drugs, human trafficking, illegal arms sales, bombings… The list goes on. The problem is they strike, and then they disappear. Sometimes the instances are days apart, sometimes they are years apart. All airports, all border checkpoints know that this group is enemy number one, yet we've never been able to identify the location of this group. And we couldn't figure out how they were getting into and out of the country so quickly."

"Now we know," I said.

"What are they called?" Emil asked.

"They call themselves K, or Kalinka. It's short for the Kaliningrad Oblast, where they hold some of their operations, but they also go by the first initial that makes up the term KGB."

"Kalinka is also the start of a delightful Russian folk song," Emil said as he brought the nearly empty shot glass to his lips, letting the last drops of liquor fall onto his tongue.

"You've never made any arrests? No raids?" I asked, perplexed by nearly 20 years of unsuccessful encounters with the organization.

"We've made some arrests in less sophisticated incidents, like car bombings, but the sons of bitches don't talk. No surprise there. We've pieced together information from separate crimes that links the events to a common source, though." Marek put out his first cigarette and lit a second one, then continued.

"I'll give you an example. In 2005, a toxic herbicide was used against northeastern farmlands. The base chemical of that herbicide, which was applied covertly by Russians hired to work the fields, was identical to a chemical we knew was developed by the Soviet Union during the Cold War. After they sprayed the fields, the

Russian farmhands left abruptly, and the fields lost all their crop that year. It put a dent in agricultural supply and, as a result, Poland had to import crop from Russia to meet commercial demands that year, making them financially dependent on their own aggressor.

"The following year, a small business emerged out of southern Poland and launched sales of incense in these premium, attractive, recyclable diffusers. They marketed themselves as the first sustainable in-home aromatherapy company in Poland, but they were still niche, and distribution was relatively low. They were a hobby shop and sold from an online boutique website. They started selling this incense, which people burned at home. The incense was produced with the same toxic chemicals used in the 2005 farmland herbicide. People were buying this stuff and inhaling it in their homes, fuming themselves to death. We probably had over one hundred reported deaths in a single week before our unit in counterintelligence at the SKW worked with the Ministry of Commerce and shut down the vendor on the site. Of course, by the time we traced them, we realized their business was registered under a dummy account and that we couldn't get to them at all."

"So, what we do now is easy, right? We report this to Polish counterintelligence, and they take out the tunnel. Fill it with concrete or something, and then we go home," I suggested. I knew I was oversimplifying it.

"You can't," Magda said. She had been silent for some time since Marek arrived at the house.

"Why not?" I asked.

"You don't want to tamper with what is in that tunnel. It's not just drugs and people they are moving through there."

"They have the control rods," Emil said. Everyone in the room turned to him, questioning his sudden and confident suggestion.

"Excuse me?" I clarified.

"Control rods to nuclear reactors. A few months ago, the Polish government reported that a high security nuclear facility called the TR-003 was broken into and the control rods, used to stabilize fission rates of the elements contained in nuclear reactors, were stolen," Emil expanded. "Don't you watch the noon news special from Warsaw every morning?"

"Poland doesn't have any nuclear power plants," I responded, crossing my arms over my chest.

"It didn't, until recently. TR-003 is a high-profile joint venture between a few of the Baltic nations. They negotiated they would share the energy generated by the plant, but now operations have been suspended due to security reasons with the stolen control rods," Marek added.

"But are the rods themselves explosive? Don't they need a corresponding reactor to function, or to pose any kind of risk of a nuclear accident? The SL-1 explosion in the 1960s and the Chernobyl disaster were because rods were being handled indelicately with the reactors, not because they broke independently." Emil spoke to Marek but then turned to Magda, who remained silent.

"Magda... Is there a nuclear reactor built underground and connected to the tunnel?" I stated what I interpreted was going through Emil's mind, which she confirmed with a nod of her head.

"I don't know what it is exactly, but the Russians have added on to the tunnel. It is expansive. They have excavated a cave and built a laboratory near the Polish entrance of the tunnel. I've only caught glimpses of it as I've entered and exited the tunnel on my runs. I don't know what's in there, but I saw them bring in the rods after the incident at the nuclear facility was reported a few months ago."

"Goddamn it," I said. My head started to spin with the facts I was learning. Every few minutes, we seemed to hear another overwhelming piece of this puzzle.

"And then there's the issue of removing individuals stationed inside or around the tunnel on Polish ground," Marek continued. "Most of them, from what we know of Kalinka's relationship with the Kremlin, are close to Medvedev, and his puppeteer, Putin. The Russians will vacate the tunnel as soon as they know a military advance is coming and deny any involvement or knowledge of it. They'll act innocent while we attack, then blame any nuclear accidents or casualties on us. If any of this affects their territory in the Kaliningrad Oblast, which, let's remember, is one kilometer from the tunnel's entrance at Café Gadam, we risk waging war on Russia."

"Do you remember the conflict in Georgia two years ago?" Emil began, looking at me from his place at the table. "Russia shoots down an unmanned Georgian drone flying over the Russian-backed Abkhazia region, then sends in waves of troops over the course of months because it claims Georgia will attack Abkhazia. Georgia, feeling the risk of an attack, sends their own troops towards South Ossetia, the other historically Russian region, and Russia responds with its own advances to that region, too. Before long, they start air strikes against the Georgians. Long story short, the result was a week-long war that resulted in hundreds of Georgians, and Russians, being killed. Most of them civilians. History proves that we need to tread lightly with them. It's 2010, not much has changed on the Eurasian continent since then."

"Emil's right. Poland has lived without direct bloodshed next to the former Soviet Union since the end of the World War II," Marek said. "We should keep it that way."

"But Georgia was part of the Soviet Union, it's different. Poland was only in its sphere of influence." I attempted to rationalize the differences between the conflicts, hoping to come to a solution. Perhaps I had bitten off more than I could chew in coming to Poland.

"Exactly. Poland will always be the one who got away for Russia." Marek agreed, lighting another cigarette. "And I'll be damned if, after a situation like Georgia, they wouldn't want to try their luck with her again."

We sat in silence for minutes in the rising clouds of smoke billowing from the lit cigarettes in the kitchen. The open window did not clear the air, and every few seconds, Magda waved her hand in front of her face until I finally extinguished my last cigarette out of sympathy.

"Okay, two questions," Emil finally spoke. "How did you put us in touch with the family of the same woman who dug the tunnel with Sosna at the end of the war? And what do we do next?"

"Coincidence, to the first question," Marek responded, leaning back in his chair. "The number of remaining people who were directly affiliated with Wachlarz is dwindling, but the network of families is still tight. Suwałki was the closest location that had someone to whom I knew you could go for medical assistance. Without knowing the details right away, I couldn't send you to a public hospital. But I had no idea you would arrive here and discover this… connection. And to the second question, I need to think."

Marek stood up with his hands on his hips, turning to the open window behind him.

"Let's go back to Warsaw," I suggested. "Any governmental entity we'd need to alert about this would be there. We could go straight to the *Służba Kontrwywiadu Wojskowego*."

"We need to be prudent before we speak to anyone about this, especially the SKW." Marek seemed hesitant, his fingers brushing over his beard as he paced.

"Are you crazy? We know that Kalinka has an illegal route into Poland and has been wreaking havoc in this country since the end of the war, and you want to sit on your hands and keep the Military Counterintelligence Service in the dark on this?" I looked up at Marek, then stood up. "I know you don't work for them anymore, but how many women have been kidnapped into prostitution rings since this tunnel has been open? How many arms have been sold on the black market and used against people in our own country? How many lives have been taken from Kalinka's crimes?"

My intent wasn't to embarrass Magda and Janina any more for their compliance with the Russians in the tunnel. Still, their eyes were cast down.

"I'm trying to show you that it is high time this is put to a stop," I said. "At the very least, release Magda from this slavery."

"You like to be bold, Joanna, but you are an heiress who has the convenience of flying back to her penthouse apartment in Chicago after this is all over, no matter how it ends," Emil replied. "Marek, Magda, Janina, and this entire country might not."

"I'll see this through. Mark my words. But we need to act on this and report it to the SKW. Marek?"

He was still facing the window, pondering the repercussions of telling our discovery to the government agency with which he was no longer associated.

"I know the people at the SKW and I know their temperaments," he stated adamantly, still looking out the window. "Their reaction to this knowledge could be catastrophic. I don't want to throw us into war."

I walked to him, facing him directly.

"That decision is not yours to make."

Our eyes met for a moment, and then I turned away, tearing my coat off my chairback and starting for the door.

"Joanna!" Emil yelled behind me and followed me as I left the house. "Where are you going?"

"Give me the keys," I spun around and extended my hand towards him, standing outside the Alfa Romeo in front of the house. "I'm going to Warsaw. I won't stand by and watch this happen. My grandfather wouldn't, either. And goddamn it, the Russians have had this war coming from us for decades. If blood will be shed, it'll be there's."

Emil stared at me, trying to sort through his reasoning in his mind, then pushed past me reluctantly and unlocked the car. He sat in the driver's seat as I made my way to the passenger door. Once I buckled myself in, I turned to look at him, searching for confirmation that he really wanted to do this.

"My grandfather made your grandfather a promise to protect him and your entire lineage for the rest of his life." He put the key in the ignition, turned the car on, and started to back out of the driveway. "If his promise was made transferrable to your father and to you, then I'm making his responsibility mine."

11

We arrived in Warsaw and headed straight to the headquarters of the SKW. The workday was nearly done and men in business suits were already exiting the building, crossing the street in pairs or small groups to the nearest bar to have a drink before dinnertime. Emil parked the car along the street. We left our guns in the glove compartment and jogged into the building.

"Ma'am, there are security protocols before entering the building," a receptionist said immediately as we walked into the atrium. We had rushed past the security guard in military uniform holding a scanner but turned around abruptly and waited in front of him. The receptionist looked at us questionably. Emil's arm was still in the sling Janina had prepared for him. He looked more like a victim than an informer.

"Do you have an appointment?" The receptionist asked as I spread my arms and legs to be scanned.

"We have an important tip. We need to speak to someone immediately," Emil said at her desk.

"I'm sorry, our directors only see individuals based on appointments, which are booked weeks in advance. They're terribly busy and, considering it is the end of the day, they might already be out."

"I am the cousin of Marek Bukowski," I attempted, hoping the name I dropped would ring a bell. Frankly, I didn't know what his exact position at the SKW was or to whom he had reported in the past. But Warsaw was a small town and, judging from his resourcefulness that day, he seemed to be well-connected. The receptionist paused and stood up. She seemed to hesitate and leaned forward, hinting silently that she knew the name.

The guard finished my scan and moved on to Emil. I sidestepped the guard and walked forward to the desk.

"Pick up the phone, dial the highest-ranking person in this office, and tell them we found Kalinka," I said sharply, lowering my voice.

"I'm sorry, I am not a field agent and don't have any knowledge of– "

"This is a matter of national security. Get me into a room with an SKW director, now."

The receptionist looked over at the guard, who nodded at her in approval. She was appalled at my bluntness, but picked up the phone, her eyes glued to me, and dialed an extension.

"Dr. Skiba? Yes, this is the reception. We have two individuals here to see you, they say they are related to Marek Bukowski…"

"Kalinka…" I whispered. The receptionist lowered her voice.

"And they say they are here in the matter of Kalinka."

She hung up the phone and walked to the staircase in the atrium. Emil and I followed her up three flights of stairs until we reached a door with a plaque that introduced Dr. Antoni Skiba to us as the Director of Field Operations for the Military Counterintelligence Service. The receptionist opened the door, allowed us inside, and closed it behind us.

Skiba sat in his leather armchair behind a long, mahogany desk, paging through papers arranged in various stacks around him. He was near the age of retirement, or perhaps past it and still tied to his job, either through passion or through his sense of duty. He wore round spectacles that reminded me of St. Maximilian Kolbe, but his elegant dark suit suggested he was less of a priest-martyr and more of a lofty office executive.

"Please, come in," he motioned to us, peering over his glasses. We approached his desk, reached over to each shake his hand, and sat down in the two chairs across from him. He screwed the cap back onto his ink fountain pen and reclined in his swiveling chair.

"Dr. Skiba, thank you for meeting with us on such short notice. I will cut to the chase, as I know you are a busy man– " I started.

"Slow down, slow down. I am in no hurry. Yes, it is 5:00 on a Tuesday afternoon, the young people are all eager to get back to their families, but this…" He gestured at the room around us. "Is a peaceful place for me. It is where I can best serve my country. So, you are Bukowskis?"

"Related to Marek Bukowski, yes. But my name is Sosna. Joanna Sosna."

"Sosna, yes, yes… The author who fought for Wachlarz, right?" Skiba clarified.

"That's right. Henryk Sosna was my grandfather. And this is Emil Łowicki, the grandchild of a close friend of my grandfather, and my childhood friend."

"Pleasure to meet you, sir," Emil said, nodding in acknowledgement.

"Likewise, likewise."

Skiba rolled his fountain pen between his hands, as if attempting to start a fire in the air. He was a slow spoken man who sounded wise without even uttering a word of wisdom. He had the time and patience to repeat the same word for emphasis, as if he were savoring it a second time.

"The receptionist mentioned Kalinka?"

"Yes, sir," I said. "We found their access point into Poland."

"Really?" Skiba stopped rolling his fountain pen between his hands, set it down on his desk, and leaned towards us. "Where?"

Emil stood up from his chair and walked to the map of Poland that Skiba had hanging on the back wall of his office, explaining the past 72 hours to the director, starting with my grandfather's funeral and ending with our departure from Suwałki. Skiba listened attentively, startled by some details and intrigued by others. He nodded along and stayed silent until Emil finished the story and sat back down in his chair. After several seconds of silence, Skiba cleared his throat and started his own monologue.

"We've been after Kalinka since I worked in the field, you know. It has been almost 20 years of terror across our country, and we know so little about them. Marek probably explained to you all there is to know about them so far. Other than a few known leads and connections across their crimes, there isn't much intelligence to act on."

"What about Magda's testimony? Their 60 years of blackmail over her? If you don't believe that there is a tunnel that runs underground and connects the three countries at the tripoint, she can take you there herself," I said, feeling anxious as I heard the same hesitation in Skiba's voice as I had in Marek's earlier that day.

"I believe you, sure, but what to do now?" Skiba asked. He was leaning back in his chair again.

"How about remove the tunnel?" I challenged him. The change in the tone of my voice caught his attention. Skiba gave a somewhat patronizing smile and looked at me across the desk.

"At the very least, I can share this tip with my colleagues, and we will see what they suggest. We can plan a slow, calculated approach to the tunnel, but we'll need to act more diplomatically than we'd like."

"Slow? Calculated? How long would that take?" Emil asked.

"Considering the levels of bureaucracy and the time it takes to get anything approved in this department of the Ministry of National Defense, maybe months. The first move will certainly be a meeting between ambassadors to see if anything can be resolved politically. That alone would take weeks to arrange."

"And you don't have a concern that Kalinka knows that we, and now the SKW, know about the access point?"

"Miss Sosna," Skiba sighed and leaned forward in his chair again, resting his forearms at the edge of his desk and folding his hands together. "There is no present threat that we need to be acting on. We take this seriously, yes, but we've also waited decades for this opportunity. We didn't know how Kalinka was getting into the country, and we didn't know if we'd ever find out. Now that we know their tactic, it needs to be confirmed, researched, and planned for accordingly. We are not involved in any kind of active conflict with Russia, and we shouldn't start one if there's any way to avoid it."

I sighed with a feeling of defeat but straightened my back so my shoulders wouldn't slump. Emil looked over at me as if for reassurance.

"How long are you in the country?" Skiba asked.

"As long as you need us to be," I responded.

"Good. Make an appointment tomorrow with the receptionist to see Jaworski, the head active field agent, for a debrief of the encounter at the tripoint. Provide descriptions of anyone you saw at Café Gadam, I'll send an agent out there early next week to run some surveillance on the place. We'll need to get a team to Suwałki and debrief Magda and Janina, too, if we think it's safe. In the meantime, you keep everything you saw and heard to yourself. Don't call anyone and don't meet with anyone unless I know of it and authorize it."

I nodded, unable to say anything else to push Skiba any harder on taking immediate action at Café Gadam.

"If it's possible, please move faster on this," Emil said, standing up from his chair.

"What makes you think we should move faster on this? Young people are so impulsive…" Skiba smiled serenely, standing up with Emil. It seemed as if he didn't feel threatened by our news of Kalinka at all.

"A granddaughter's intuition," I responded, the last one to stand in the room.

"Poetic, poetic… Well, we will be seeing you around headquarters here over the next week. Jaworski will update me on the debrief and if we need anything more from you."

"Thank you, Dr. Skiba," I said coldly, turning to the door. I had the greatest respect for the military and national defense, naturally, but I sensed that both Marek and Skiba were being imprudent.

Emil and I left the SKW building and, as soon as I stepped outside, I lit a cigarette.

"Drink?" Emil asked.

"Yeah."

"There's a place off Nowy Świat that's good."

"Too mainstream. Let's go to Praga. There's a place with a view of the river you'd like."

12

We were seated outside on a terrace, surrounded by heated lamps. Despite the spring chill, we welcomed the outdoors after a day in the car, and our table was made even more comfortable with a virgin wool blanket draped over the back of every chair. We ordered vodka cocktails, oysters with horseradish and lemon, and cabbage croquettes with mushroom sauce, then reclined with a view of the Vistula, illuminated along its banks, before us.

"When was the last time you were here?" Emil asked. I was thrilled to discuss anything but the disappointment with Skiba.

"In Poland? Just last year. I took a short sabbatical and stayed along the Baltic in a hotel near Gdańsk," I said, sipping from the martini glass. "And you?"

"It's been too long… Four, maybe five years? I was here doing research for a doctoral paper I was writing at the time."

"Writing and more writing for you."

"One day, when I'm less busy teaching in Boston, I want to have a place of my own here. There are these historic condos that have been renovated in Kraków. My friend owns one and loves it there."

I tried not to let myself get lost in the chain of thoughts that erupted in my mind of living in Poland with Emil. Owning a city condo surrounded by centuries-old buildings, walking together for cappuccinos, reading in bed until the late morning, smoking at night on the rooftops under the stars…

I changed the subject before I became too optimistic.

"I read your book that you co-wrote on the Battle of Monte Cassino and the II Corps, you know. It was very good. I think I learned more about General Władysław Anders from you than from any of my Polish Saturday School teachers growing up."

"What a high pedestal you put me on, Joanna," Emil joked, finishing the remaining drink in his glass.

"What can I say? You're an impressive man."

"Not more impressive than you. 30 years old and already the CFO of a mining company?"

"I had an in with the company from Dziadek, you know that. But at least now I know why he got into mining."

"To inherit a position is one thing, to maintain it is another."

"It's hardly putting my education to any good use. I'm signing approvals for wire transfers, mostly, instead of studying differential equations. If I had gone into engineering, at least my education would be applicable to the company. And perhaps now, this tunnel."

"You're well-rounded. History, business, mathematics… *La femme nouvelle*."

I caught his eye, his face radiant from the candlelight on the table. My heart skipped a beat as he winked, but just then, my cell phone rang from the pocket of my parka. I rolled my eyes, wishing we hadn't been interrupted, and hopefully signaling to Emil that I wanted that moment between us to last a bit longer.

"It's probably just your grandfather," I said with a sigh. I took my phone and checked the screen for the caller. "It's… Marek."

Emil cocked his head to the side and leaned over the table towards me.

"Pick it up."

"Hello?" I answered the call.

"Joanna, it's Marek. Magda and Janina are dead."

"Oh my God… How?"

"After you left, I went up to Café Gadam to clear my head after we talked and maybe look around myself. Magda and Janina told me to be back for dinner before I returned to Warsaw. When I came back to their house, they were already dead. Shot in the chest."

"Goddamn it. Kalinka got to them," I said. Emil realized what was happening without hearing Marek's side of the conversation and ran his hand through his thick hair, sighing with frustration.

"Shit…" He whispered across the table.

"Did you report it?" I asked Marek.

"And say what? Tell the local police that a quasi-terrorist Russian organization that has been penetrating our borders since the end of the war killed two innocent women in a rural village?" Marek asked frantically.

"So they're just laying in their house, dead?"

"Listen, take my advice. Don't get any more involved in this than you already are. Take Emil and go home tomorrow morning. You don't want these people to find you, too." Marek was avoiding my question.

"I'll talk to Emil," I said, and hung up on Marek. I tossed my phone onto the table. "Change of plans."

"We can't go back to his place tonight," he said to me across the table immediately. In the chaotic trip we had already had, I was comforted by his ability to think at the same pace as I did. I knew I didn't need to explain anything to him.

"I know that," I said. "Marek might be compromised."

"I don't like how close he was to the deaths of Magda and Janina after they had just divulged their deepest secrets to us," Emil said, voicing my doubts out loud. "So where to?"

"Hotel La Pologne. It's in Old Town, we will have to make our way there to see if there's room tonight."

Emil tossed a few banknotes onto the table, covering our drinks and meal and leaving plenty as tip for the waiter. We pulled on our parkas, left the restaurant, and boarded a cab parked on the street at the commercial front.

The cab pulled up to the ornate, French-inspired hotel in the most picturesque quarter of Warsaw. The boutique hotel was snuggled between a jazz club and a bakery with a view of the illuminated Royal Castle that sat at the end of a street called Krakowskie Przedmieście. The castle was the regal introduction to the Old Town quarter, which had been, like the rest of the capital, desecrated to the ground during the 1944 Warsaw Uprising, but later beautifully rebuilt. I loved Old Town and its resemblance to Prague in its burnt red rooftops and colorful building façades. It was Warsaw's main attraction for tourists, but it was one of my favorite places in the world. It represented the resurrection of the entire country following the war, rising like a phoenix from its ashes. It was not just a charming Eastern European city; it was hope incarnate.

We paid the cab driver and walked through the sliding glass doors into the hotel lobby, lush with grandiose bouquets on the coffee tables.

"*Dobry wieczór,*" I greeted the woman at the reception. "Is there any possibility we could book two rooms for tonight?"

"*Dobry wieczór.* Let me see…" She scrolled through the rooming availability on her desktop monitor, and then shook her head at the screen. "I'm sorry, the only room we have available is the Palatial King Suite."

"That will work," Emil interrupted, handing the receptionist a credit card. A sweat broke out on my forehead, as I processed Emil's forward gesture in booking a hotel room for us both.

"Very well. How many nights?"

"We'll be staying indefinitely," I said.

"Our pleasure. And may our attendant help you with your bags?" The receptionist said, entering our payment information into her computer.

"We haven't any," I responded, remembering that Emil still wore his sling. She probably thought we had recently escaped a crime scene.

"Oh! Allow us to bring a basket of personal essentials to your room, compliments of Hotel La Pologne."

"Thank you," I said, relieved that I wouldn't have to spend the night in the same room as Emil without access to a toothbrush.

"Room number 12 on the top floor, the staircase to your right will bring you to your suite," the woman motioned the directions for us and handed us each a keycard.

"*Dziękujemy bardzo*," Emil and I thanked her in unison, then ascended the stairs.

13

I believed I knew Emil better than anyone in the world. When we were young, our families were always together, and as the only children of our parents, we were always together. He was my best friend for as long as I could remember, and with every summer spent in Poland, we seemed to become closer.

He challenged me in a way no one could. When he won the Greater Chicago History Competition in eighth grade, I decided I needed to win the International Junior Math League Final that same year. When he hit every bullseye in target practice at self-defense camp during archery week the summer after senior year of high school, I made sure to do the same during pistol week. Mine were moving targets.

The area where we diverged were in our relationships with people. He was able to lure in any woman he wanted, while I hesitated with men. I often felt they were unsatisfied by my ability to humble myself to create any kind of interpersonal connection. As one ex-boyfriend said to me before leaving my condo for the last time, I was a "seductive but egotistical bitch." A few of those words were accurate about me, but then again, he probably became frustrated because it was quite clear that he was not the brightest of the pair. He had some choice words about my inheritance and my "haughty" quality of life, too. He tried to make his departure personal.

The only thing my past relationships taught me were that I wasn't personable, but now that I was entering the most elegant room of the grandest hotel in Warsaw with Emil, I realized that I perhaps just wasn't personable with the right people. With him, my barriers seemed to fall away. I didn't need to humble myself to his level because he was already on mine.

The heavy door closed behind us, but before either of us could say a word to each other, someone knocked. Emil peeked through the peephole and pulled open the door. An attendant stood outside with a brass cart on top of which sat two crystal wine glasses and a golden bucket cradling a bottle of Saint-Émilion. On the second shelf of the cart, a wicker basket with a white napkin lining held the personal essentials the receptionist mentioned would be delivered. I was just as relieved to see the dental kits, hairbrushes, deodorant, and makeup remover as I was the charming drink. I thought I even caught a glimpse of French perfume samples at the rim of the basket.

"Compliments of the hotel, sir," the attendant reported. Emil handed him a banknote, thanked him, and allowed him inside to roll in the cart. The attendant set the basket on a side table and left. We were once again alone.

"Marek is compromised, Magda is dead, Skiba won't listen to us," Emil thought out loud as he popped open the bottle of wine. He did it as if he had done it a thousand times before. Emil had taken his coat off and had unwrapped his sling from earlier that day, and he now moved his injured arm with ease. He handed me a glass and looked at me with such confidence that I thought he had forgotten about the blood-stained shoulder of his sweater.

"So now all we have is each other," I said, clinking glasses with him and sipping the bold merlot in time with him.

"I don't mind that arrangement at all," he replied. Emil stepped towards me. His voice sounded lower, almost husky.

Emil lowered the glass from his lips, setting it on the side table behind him. He ran his fingers through my hair behind my head, then brought my face to his, pressing his lips against mine. It was intentional, he made sure I understood that, kissing me long and hard, then again, and again. And I, with all my intentionality, kissed him back.

We undressed each other as if we were running out of time, and spent the rest of the night intertwined, moving from the bed to the couch to the table to the floor. I realized I had waited my entire adult life for him to take me. That night, in what I considered the most stunning city, I had no problem letting him do just that.

~ ~ ~

The morning sunlight fell into our room through the doors of our terrace, which overlooked the main square of the Royal Castle. I woke up to the bright room and, reminding myself that Emil was asleep beneath the sheets next to me, I walked to the doors, pulling back the white linen curtains to look outside. I had seen the square lit up the night before, but the morning in Warsaw was completely different. Shopkeepers were setting up their storefronts and the soft music from the accordionist sitting outside the bakery next to the hotel drifted up to our window. I opened one of the doors and breathed in the fresh spring air, letting the breeze enter the room and settle on my bare skin.

I called the bakery and ordered two espressos, a selection of pastries, and the morning newspaper, which were delivered to our door within minutes, then went into the expansive bathroom. I filled the bathtub with steaming hot water and set my espresso cup on the vanity. I settled into the bathtub, then pulled open the newspaper, starting with the *Polityka* section.

"Miss Sosna," Emil's familiar, still husky voice said from outside the bathroom door. I smiled as he walked into the bathroom in his briefs, exposing his chiseled body, as if Michelangelo's David was walking towards me. Every part of him looked just as alluring as it had the night before and it took self-control to stay in the tub rather than escaping, completely soaked, to repeat last night's events.

"Mister Łowicki," I replied, taking a sip of my espresso. I saw he had already found his on the table in the suite. Emil leaned over the edge of the bathtub and pulled my face in for a long kiss.

"Ready for another day of solving your grandfather's mysteries?"

"Only with you," I said.

"What's new this morning in the fatherland?" Emil asked, his eyes scanning my body through the water. The bubbles collected at my breasts and at my bent knees.

"A couple of local robberies, a new cabaret opening in the city center, and the market is up," I reported.

"Busy day in Warsaw," Emil noted sarcastically. "I just called the SKW. The earliest they can get us an appointment is Friday morning."

"Two days from now?" I asked, setting my cup down on the saucer.

"Skiba didn't seem enthusiastic about making this Kalinka discovery a priority, maybe Jaworski will. But that only means that you and I have the next two days in Warsaw all to ourselves."

"We do both need the vacation…"

"Let's walk Nowy Świat today and get ourselves some new clothes. You need a nice evening dress for tonight."

"Tonight?"

"I forgot that I had another contact at the SKW. We could try counterintelligence from a different angle and see what he says."

"Skiba said not to talk to anyone without his permission."

"And Skiba isn't helping us move anything any more quickly. We don't have anything better to do until Friday."

"Who is it?"

"He's not quite as high up as Skiba, but he's well-connected. He was the only other Pole that studied at Oxford in my graduating class. We didn't speak to each other too much, but we were close enough to exchange phone numbers. He's in the Laboratory Division within the Science and Technology Branch. He might be able to tell us more about the control rods."

"It's worth a shot."

"We'll get changed and then we'll spend the day on the town," Emil leaned over to kiss me again, then left the bathroom, stealing one last look before he closed the door.

14

We came back to the hotel after an entire day of shopping and sipping wine across the city. Our paper bags were filled with everything from lingerie to heels to men's suits. I was relieved to have a full closet of comfortable clothes again, considering our suitcases had been abandoned at my cousin's condo the night before.

My phone rang just as I walked into the bathroom to start getting ready for dinner that evening. It was Agata.

"Emil!" I called from the bathroom sink.

"Yes?"

"Agata's calling. She's going to want to know why we didn't come home yesterday."

"Tell her the truth," Emil said, stepping into the bathroom, leaning against the door frame.

"That we think her husband is conspiring with a post-KGB organization that's terrorizing the country?"

"No," Emil walked to me and stood behind me, one hand on my hip, the other brushing my hair away from my ear as he kissed the side of my neck. "That we needed some time alone to get to know each other better."

I smiled at the sentiment but gently redirected the conversation to the issue at hand.

"Do you think she knows about Marek?"

"I don't know, but either way, it's a believable story. Just text her," he said, kissing my neck one more time, then leaving the bathroom.

I typed out a convincing story on my phone, but then realized that, like Emil said, I was not lying to her at all. I sent the text, then returned to my preparation for the evening.

~ ~ ~

An hour later, I emerged from the bathroom in polished black stilettos and a backless black Ossoliński dress, my hair pulled back into a low sleek bun. The echo of my heels tapping against the marble flooring of our suite summoned Emil from our bedroom, and he appeared in his dark tailored suit. We convinced the hesitant tailor of same-day service when I slipped him a rolled-up wad of a thousand *złoty* at the measurement appointment. He suddenly didn't think that prioritizing our order for that evening would be an issue at all.

Emil and I made our way to the agreed upon club closer to the city's financial district. It was a place further away from our hotel so our dinner guest wouldn't know where we were staying should anything go awry with him. The club would also be louder than the average restaurant so we could discuss sensitive matters without risking anyone eavesdropping on us.

When we arrived at the club, I followed Emil past the guards, who nodded at us to enter, and down a set of stairs leading from the main road into a basement. The outside doors to the club were remarkably soundproof, restricting the heavy bass coming from inside the establishment from trickling out to the public. It was dark inside, with soft blue uplights along the cement perimeter of the basement. Elevated booths in the lower seating area were completely occupied by men in black suits, sprinkled around the venue like a sea of penguins, and women in lowcut dresses, peacocking for each other. For a Wednesday night in Warsaw, it seemed like this was where all the animals met when they came out at night.

Emil and I walked towards the one booth where a single man sat. Ever the scientist, he wore khaki pants and a dark green parka, ignoring any dress code for the club. I was surprised he was allowed into the building dressed like that, but the people who knew about this place seemed to be those with money. I expected they could get past the bouncers wearing anything they wanted, whether or not it conformed to the financial district's expectations. We wove around the tables in the lower seating area, through the smoky air, until we arrived at his table.

"Mister Golecki," Emil greeted the scientist at the booth. I could barely hear his introduction over the booming mellow electronic beat.

"Mister Łowicki," he responded. The man was young, thin, and short. Behind his glasses, he looked too meek to be sitting at a club on a weeknight. Within seconds of meeting him, it was evident he was suppressing frantic mannerisms. It was 8:00 in the evening and he seemed in a hurry to be somewhere, his eyes darting past our shoulders around the club. Or perhaps he was just nervous to be seen with us.

"Joanna, this is Grzegorz Golecki. Golecki, this is Joanna Sosna, I told you about her over the phone," Emil introduced me. I stood up to shake hands.

"Pleased to meet you, Mister Golecki. Thank you for joining us on such short notice."

"Yes, yes. Well, I am a busy man and have an appointment at 9:00," he checked his watch for the time. "So, let's order drinks promptly and discuss this issue of yours."

I felt compelled to move along with the agenda for that evening, so I sat down first, and folded my hands in my lap. I wasn't offended by his blunt approach to the topic. We all knew we weren't at the club to exchange niceties and small talk.

"We believe we know who stole the nuclear rods in January of this year from the power plant near Ukraine that has since been shut down," Emil started, speaking as discretely as he could while also making sure he was heard over the music.

"The TR-003 power plant? Impossible," he said. The waiter approached as we put in our drink and dinner orders.

"Does the word Kalinka mean anything to you?" I asked, watching as the waiter walked away. I had lowered my voice, but my volume adjustment seemed unnecessary, as I struggled to even hear the waiter speaking to us across the table moments earlier.

"Everyone at the SKW knows about Kalinka. We just don't have many details on their organization. Why?"

"Emil and I believe we found their entry point into Poland. We think they have the control rods."

"Interesting. Go on."

"It's a long story, but I'll be brief. After my grandfather's funeral on Saturday, I was followed by a spy, for lack of better term. We interrogated him in Chicago. With a little bit of digging, we eventually were led to the tripoint area at the coordinates where Poland, Lithuania, and the Kaliningrad Oblast meet in the north. There's a small shack there, publicly called Café Gadam, which is a discrete commercial cover for a tunnel whose excavation dates back to 1945. My grandfather led the project to build that tunnel after the war, but it was recouped by the Soviets near its completion. The entire excavation team was assassinated upon Soviet discovery, except for my grandfather and a woman named Magda."

"A tunnel? Manmade?" Golecki clarified as he received his drink, a Pepsi, from the waiter.

"We didn't go inside because as soon as the security, disguised as restaurant staff, realized we weren't average customers, they attacked, and we escaped. But we confirmed the tunnel with Magda, who we encountered afterwards by sheer coincidence. She has been a mule for Kalinka for over 60 years. They've leveraged her from the start. Kalinka has been selling arms, facilitating human trafficking, and transporting drugs by way of the tunnel since they gained control of it."

"How long is the tunnel?"

"It's set up in a V shape connecting the three countries, Magda said, with the vertex at Café Gadam. Each leg is about one or two kilometers long, just enough to get over the national borders," Emil explained, sipping the whiskey he received from the waiter.

"This is extremely advanced... It is hard to believe this exists, but incredible things happened towards the end of the war, especially on the eastern front. They must have improvised soil conditioning. And who knows how they cut through rocks. How was the tunnel reinforced? This was 65 years ago. Tunnel excavation would have been extremely rudimentary. But if they had a few brilliant minds in the mining field, perhaps they managed something. I'm surprised it hasn't collapsed yet."

"We don't know the answers, and we won't know, unless we go there ourselves. Magda was shot dead in her own home with her only living daughter after we left their house yesterday," I said.

"Good lord."

"We brought a gift for you, too," Emil said, laying the plastic bag of shrapnel that Janina had removed from his shoulder on the table. "Run analytics on this material and see if it matches up with anything in your system."

"Gladly," Golecki said, stuffing the bag promptly into the pocket of his jacket. "The more we have documented on Kalinka and anything it uses, the better. Alright, so what about these rods?"

Golecki seemed astounded by our story so far, but engaged. He had nearly finished his Pepsi. I wondered if his frenetic movements were social habits or just fueled by caffeine.

"Magda said that Kalinka has added on to the tunnel and has created what she called a laboratory underground. She claims that at the same time the nuclear rods were stolen from TR-003, they were brought into the lab."

"Son of a bitch. If you can't see it from the earth's surface, then they've made a small modular reactor." Finally, his scientific background was beginning to surface.

"A what?" Emil asked.

"It's probably the first of its kind in the entire world. Scientists have been working on it for some time, and we knew the Russians were close to finishing a proof of concept. The field thought it was years into the future before it could be achieved. An SMR is a fraction of the size of a full-blown nuclear power plant. It's very efficient. It can be scaled up or down depending on the demand for energy. It's much cheaper to build, though if we are dealing with Kalinka, investment isn't a problem for them. The control rods, at least the ones used at TR-003, are filled with boron and command the rate of fission against the reactor's uranium. Without them, you don't have a functioning reactor."

"Why position a nuclear reactor there, of all places?" Emil asked Golecki.

"Energy supply to the Baltic states is my only guess," Golecki proposed. "Kalinka establishes its own power generation, it reaches Poland, Lithuania, Latvia, Estonia, and maybe even Belarus and beyond. I don't know how sophisticated the underground plant is, but it must be massive to be able to do that. The energy would be cleaner, more efficient. The national governments contract with the lowest rates on the market and let other energy companies go out of business."

"Complete market takeover. Probably masked by some shell company to keep Kalinka anonymous," I expanded.

"Or not so anonymous," Golecki suggested.

"Are you suggesting the governments of the Baltic states are aware that they're dealing with a faction of the former KGB?" I asked.

"I'm suggesting that in order for an arrangement like that to work, Kalinka would need to have a contact inside each government, inside each Ministry of Energy, who is approving the deals. Government contracts are extremely sensitive and subject to audits, investigations, you name it. I don't see how this would work if Kalinka didn't have a mole within every nation they supply power to."

"There's nothing illicit about nuclear energy supply, though," Emil added. "There's no reason the Russians would need to keep something like that secret, if energy is distributed fairly and it can be regulated by the nations receiving it."

"Yes, but a nuclear reactor is vulnerable enough that if someone were to strike at it, the collateral damage would be catastrophic. We're talking about another Chernobyl," Golecki responded. "A nuclear reactor is already sensitive in itself, but the control rods are even more delicate. Most nuclear power plants today don't even allow for human manipulation of control rods. They're completely administered by computers."

"The reactor is a red herring," I said slowly, pausing to rationalize Kalinka's strategy. "It's safeguarding the tunnel."

"It's only placed there so the tunnel stays intact. They've protected the tunnel by making the reactor untouchable. On a chessboard, it's the queen guarding the king," Emil added.

"You're right. The way I see it, if someone were to ever discover the tunnel, like you did, they would be blinded by the reactor. From my understanding, the only reason you know of the crimes Kalinka is carrying out is because you stumbled upon Magda," Golecki took a sip of his Pepsi just as the waiter brought us our food.

"Exactly," I said, starting to eat my pad thai.

"So what did the SKW say?" Golecki asked, taking a bite of his salad.

"We went straight to Skiba," Emil started.

"Good choice."

"He won't budge," Emil finished his thought with another sip of his whiskey.

"What?" Golecki looked up, shocked, and set his fork down.

"He admits there's too much bureaucracy to step over and not enough reason to act hastily," I added.

"If he doesn't think that stolen nuclear rods being used to undermine other energy companies in the Baltic region, much less the other crimes you described, is reason to act, then perhaps it's time for him to finally retire," Golecki said.

"We have a meeting set up with Jaworski on Friday morning, but other than that, we are stuck," I said.

"If you want, I'll do what I can to report this up the chain from my side."

"Skiba forbade us from speaking to anyone about this. We have to wait to speak to Jaworski," Emil disagreed.

"I wish we didn't have to adhere to protocol."

Golecki picked up his fork again and ate the remainder of his meal quickly. Emil and I looked at each other, but no exchange of glances could communicate what either of us should say next. Even if Golecki were willing to help us, it seemed we had just exhausted our last resource at the SKW.

15

Golecki called us the next morning. He confirmed that the shrapnel Emil provided to him, when dimensionally recreated as a digital rendering of a bullet, matched a bullet that had been used in a 2008 mass shooting at one of the largest shopping centers in Warsaw. The shooting, which killed 10 people, was presumed to have been coordinated by Kalinka as a distraction from an ancillary raid of a university laboratory where nuclear research in preparation for TR-003 had been underway. If nothing else we mentioned last night would have convinced Golecki of our discovery of Kalinka, the results of the analytics on the shrapnel we gave to him were enough.

Emil and I spent the rest of that following day walking the city in hopes of distracting ourselves from the impending Jaworski meeting and dissecting the encounter at Café Gadam and

Magda's house. We assumed we would be debriefed separately, so we prepared our statements ahead of time to make sure our accounts were aligned.

We finally arrived at the offices of the SKW on Friday morning, Emil dressed in a navy suit and I in a grey one-piece jumpsuit with a blazer draped over my shoulders. It was a characteristically dreary day, as most of the week had been, so we hurried under an umbrella into the same atrium we had visited on Tuesday.

Jaworski was half an hour late to our debrief and, as expected, we were interviewed separately. I went first for two hours, then waited for Emil to finish his turn. We compared the questions we were asked, discovering that they were the same ones. Times of departures and arrivals, identifications of the armed men at Café Gadam, the discussions between us and Magda, and all other details that Jaworski asked us were promptly disclosed with full cooperation. At the end of my debrief, I had asked what else the SKW might need from me or Emil.

"Nothing, I think you can continue on your Polish vacation," he responded with a satisfied tone. He seemed to have gotten everything he needed from me. "You aren't an agent with us, there is little you can do now. We will take it from here."

By the time the debriefs concluded, it was time for *obiad*, the mid-afternoon meal, which preceded a later supper. Emil seemed as exhausted as I was after the meetings. It was more of a moral defeat rather than a physical expenditure that wore us out. We decided to dine at a traditional restaurant to indulge in some of the last authentic Polish food before our potential departure for Chicago the next day.

"Are you sure you want to go back already?" Emil asked as he began eating his red borscht. It was a bold meal choice considering the pressed white shirt he wore underneath his suit jacket. I didn't need to remind him of the risk of staining his clothes. He already knew, so he tucked his napkin into his collar like a bib. He was raised by a good Polish mother.

"What else can we do? Skiba and Golecki won't help us and we're worried that Marek is implicated because of his proximity to Magda and Janina's deaths. What are we going to do now, call 112?" I asked, starting my own appetizer of hot chicken soup. "They'd probably disregard us like everyone else has, and the police certainly won't move any faster than counterintelligence."

"Let's just enjoy the rest of tonight and, in the morning, if you still feel the same way, we will book our return flight. How does that sound?" Emil asked.

Part of me wanted to stay in this sweet homeland that had become even more significant to me, allowing Emil and I all the time we needed to reacquaint ourselves with each other. We'd fly back to Chicago, he would finish out his spring break at home, and then return to Harvard's campus to continue what he had been doing before – teaching and writing.

The other part of me was tired from the fairy tale we had been living that week and, vanquished by the empty promises of potential governmental intervention into the issue of the tunnel, wanted to go home anyway. I realized that the next day marked the one-week anniversary of my grandfather's funeral, which further explained my tiredness and need to rest at home.

"Okay," I finally agreed. The events of the past week were still on my mind, but I refocused my attention to the present moment, and the rest of that blissful night, promenading the streets of Warsaw with Emil.

16

The next morning began just as every morning had that week in the Palatial King Suite of Hotel La Pologne, only with a much later start. Emil and I had spent the previous evening talking, drinking, and even playing cards with a new deck we bought from a souvenir shop in an alley of an Old Town street. We went through the litany of games my grandfather had taught us, ending the night with the least demanding of all the games – War. Drunk from the excess of vodka we had consumed throughout the night in the room, I couldn't remember the time we had fallen asleep. It couldn't have been earlier than 4:00 in the morning. Naturally, our Saturday was delayed.

I awoke first, the sheets twisted around my body, lying next to Emil. I crawled out of bed to open the terrace doors and then ordered our daily espresso, pastries, and newspaper from the bakery. I pulled on the robe that rested on the armchair next to the bed and checked the time on my watch – 1:15. Clearly, our bodies and minds needed the rest if we had slept into the afternoon.

Someone outside the door knocked. The attendant normally waited for me in the hallway, accepting his generous tip giddily, but that morning, the tray waited for me alone and the attendant was nowhere to be seen. I retrieved the tray with the goods I had ordered, the newspaper laying on top. On any normal morning, the headlining photo on the front page would have been a picture of the president, prime minister, or a member of parliament, surrounded by text summarizing the latest gossip around their political agenda.

That morning, I found myself looking at a page-wide picture of a destroyed airplane lying in a wooded area, smoke still rising from its detritus. I set the tray on the coffee table before I could drop it from shock and picked up the gazette in my hands. The headline at the top of the front page was written in perhaps the largest font the editor could demand. As if screaming from the paper I was holding, the text read *KATASTROFA W SMOLEŃSKU*.

Catastrophe in Smoleńsk.

My eyes scanned the subtext of the headline in disbelief. The list of victims looked to be almost one-hundred names long. The first two names were Lech and Maria Kaczyński.

The president and first lady of Poland had been killed in a plane crash.

I kept reading in horror as the prominent names of Polish public figures were listed out in alphabetical order. Among them were the last president of the Polish government in exile, members of parliament, and the deputy marshal of the Sejm and the Senate. The list couldn't seem to end.

"Emil," I said softly as I read the rest of the page. Realizing he was a much harder sleeper than I was, I tried again. "Emil!"

"What?" He asked groggily, rolling out of bed. After not hearing a response from me, he walked into the living room where I sat holding the newspaper on the velvet couch.

"There's been a plane crash…" I started, handing him the paper. I was speechless. I let him read the front page before saying a word.

"…the representatives of the Polish government were flying to Smoleńsk, Russia on the 70th anniversary of the Katyń Massacre to commemorate the victims of the war atrocity. Initial reports deem poor visibility and foggy weather conditions to be the cause of the crash. No survivors have been found at this time…"

"What do you think?" I asked. "You do realize that nearly every political leader in any position of power is now dead."

"Shit," Emil said, throwing the paper on the ground and walking to the terrace door. "The government is completely exposed."

"We discovered Kalinka's tunnel and a week later, the Polish president and ninety-something other representatives of the government are killed in a plane crash in Russia?"

"I know."

"Please don't tell me I'm crazy to think that this is not a coincidence." I kept my eyes on Emil as he paced on the opposite side of the couch, and then turned my head back to the newspaper to give him some time to absorb the information. As I went to pick it up from the floor, I saw a small slip of white folded notebook paper peeking from between the pages of the newspaper. My hands began to sweat as I lifted it to my lap and opened it.

Go home.
K.

I began to shake. Emil turned as he paced, then walked over to me when he noticed I was holding the note. He read it to himself, then dropped his hands to his sides in exasperation.

"We can get out of this. Kalinka is giving us an out right now, Joanna. The next flight out of Warsaw leaves in two hours, we just need to get ourselves to Chopin International and forget about all of this."

"And just leave Kalinka to slowly whittle away at this entire country? Do you realize we are the only ones who know about the tunnel and are motivated enough to do something about it?"

"This is serious, Joanna. This isn't some spy game. This could be a declaration of war."

"I know," I said, standing up and tightening the cloth rope around the waist of my robe. "And if it's war, I'm fighting."

My adamant stance made Emil sigh again, knowing he couldn't back out of staying with me based on his promise he made in the car earlier that week as we were leaving Suwałki.

"Fine," Emil said, collapsing into the velvet couch. I traded places with him and stood at the terrace doors, staring outside. The square in front of the Royal Castle was bustling that afternoon. It was a Saturday, so only retailers were working, but the chatter amongst those walking the city that afternoon looked to be frantic. I watched as arms waved passionately through conversations that small groups were having. Older men pointed to the sky, incredulously recounting the recent events in Russia to their colleagues. Warsaw, like me, was freshly in awe.

"Emil, you don't think it's strange that Skiba and Jaworski stalled us for so long this week?" I asked. My eyes remained on the people in the square.

"In the same way Marek was stalling us?"

"Yes."

"I suppose their reaction was consistent with his response, yes."

"And we have reason to believe Marek killed Magda and Janina, right? He wanted to eliminate two of the four living non-Kalinka people who knew about the tunnel?"

"Or at least was somehow involved in it. I certainly wouldn't trust him right now."

"I think Skiba is in on it. I think the SKW is compromised."

"It's a bold assumption, Joanna, to think that the Director of Field Operations for the Military Counterintelligence Service knew about and condoned a plane crash. The president of the same country he works for is now dead."

"I know. But my intuition was right before." I stepped away from the terrace door and sat down slowly next to Emil, finally taking a sip of my espresso. I realized I had a pounding headache from my hangover but was too preoccupied with the newspaper and Kalinka's note to care.

"So now what?" Emil asked, grabbing a raspberry danish from the tray on the coffee table.

"I think we need to get to the tripoint again. And we need someone who can help us with the rods."

"Golecki?"

"Do you have a better idea?"

"So, we kidnap Golecki, drive to the tripoint, get past the heavily guarded entrance to the tunnel, and then what? Override the computer-controlled reactor to remove the rods and detonate two kilometers of underground tunnel?"

"That's not a bad idea, actually."

"Joanna, we're going home. We cannot do this. We don't have enough people, nor are we professionally trained. There will be an international investigation of the crash site, the world will see that it was Russia who caused it–"

"And then what? Economic sanctions? We've seen how well that has worked in diplomatic relations with Russia. And if you think Russia will allow an investigation of the site, that's bullshit. It's on their territory. They might conduct their own, but they have a cover for their story, as you saw in the newspaper. Weather conditions. You want to go home, and you'd feel comfortable sitting in Boston watching the news unfold on your TV as Poland becomes another Georgia?"

We both sighed and stayed silent for a moment. I pulled out my phone to scroll through my news apps and continued reading updates on the plane crash. After a few moments, I noticed that not much information was available since the incident had occurred just an hour earlier.

Sitting on the couch, I ran through the events of the week in my mind and paused on the death of Magda and Janina. Curious about their funeral, I navigated on my phone's browser to what looked like the website of Suwałki's main newspaper and tapped through the page until I reached the Obituaries section. I read her memorial out loud in Polish.

"Jaros, Magda. 92 years old. Passed away on Tuesday, April 6, 2010 in her home. Fervent patriot and veteran field nurse of the Wachlarz armed resistance organization during World War II. Devoted mother. Survived by daughter, Janina Jaros…"

"What did you just say?" Emil asked. He ripped the phone from my hand to see the last line of the obituary himself.

"Janina's alive?"

~ ~ ~

We showered and changed into our clothes, then made our way to a public payphone outside the hotel. Kalinka knew where we were staying, and we were desperate to leave our hotel room as soon as we could.

We spent the morning calling medical centers near Suwałki, assuming that if Marek had shot Magda, then Janina would have somehow been seriously injured, too. Fortunately for us, Poland's medical confidentiality regulations were far below the American HIPAA standards, and with a few white lies told to hospital receptionists over the phone about our relation to Janina, we finally reached the phoneline of her hospital room. We were advised that she wasn't yet completely lucid from the painkillers and shock of that week.

"You have no idea how happy I am to hear that you're still here," Janina said weakly over the phone. Emil and I huddled in the phone booth and shared the receiver, increasing the volume to its maximum level and listening to her voice together.

"We are so sorry for the loss of your mother," I said.

"It was Marek," Janina whispered.

"We knew he was compromised. He called us after he shot you and told us you were both dead. We think he was trying to scare us out of the country and mind our own business," I explained.

"He certainly tried to kill us. He shot us both. Mama didn't make it. She was shot in the chest and died on the spot. He shot me in the stomach, and was going to pull the trigger again, but was interrupted when my neighbor started making his way to our house. You could hear the gunshots outside."

"We saw you were still alive when we read Magda's obituary," Emil said.

"I'll be just fine, but you need to get to the tripoint," Janina replied.

"We were already planning on it. What do we do when we get there? You know more about this tunnel from your mother's activity in it than we do."

"After you left our house on Tuesday, Mama told me that the plane crash was an operation they had been planning for several months. It wasn't supposed to happen for quite some time, but they felt rushed into the operation after you discovered the tunnel. They accelerated the timetable, and the commemoration trip that was supposed to happen this morning in Smoleńsk was a perfect opportunity for them to wipe out the most prominent figures in the government and they made it look like an accident," Janina explained slowly through gasps of air. We could hear her suffering in her voice.

"Why didn't she say anything while we were there? Why haven't you said anything to the authorities since Tuesday?"

"Mama had seen Marek at Café Gadam in the past. She didn't want to expose what she knew in front of him."

"And you?"

"You've probably noticed by now that most of the higher-ranking officials at the SKW are corrupt, no?" Janina asked.

"Yes."

"There's rot growing throughout the entire government like this, Joanna." A beep came through the phone, warning me of the time elapsed, so I dropped another coin into the slot to continue the conversation.

"How?" I asked.

"In order to facilitate communism's collapse in Poland, many politicians had to make compromises at the Round Table Agreement in 1989, where representatives of the communist government as well as the Solidarity trade union met to resolve their differences. As you know, the result of the Round Table Agreement was a democratic Poland. But some of the people who had rubbed shoulders with the communists, and even the Soviets, remained in positions of power in the new country," Janina coughed, took a few shaky breaths, then continued. "That was the only way the Round Table Agreement could come to the resolution that it eventually did. A bicameral legislature, a democratically elected president, the legalization of the Solidarity trade union… all of it was possible and agreed to by the communists because the anti-communists had to make some concessions."

"Was Skiba one of the former communists?" Emil asked.

"One of many. Those who remained in the newly created government kept low profiles with the communists through 1989, so most of the public was unaware of their dealings. It kept both sides happy. The anti-communists got their democracy, and the communists got to stay, most of them unpunished for the transgressions they had carried out against their country in the past. And the public remained in blissful ignorance, absorbing the benefits of their new, free country."

"So what do we do now?" I asked.

"The politicians inside the Polish government, Skiba, Marek, the people approving nuclear energy supply from the tunnel's reactors, and anyone else that's corrupt is on Kalinka's payroll. They carry out Kalinka's commands and then are compensated for it. Whoever caused the plane to crash this morning in Smoleńsk was one of them. And if a coup were to ever take place and Russia were to secure Poland, they would retain their roles, or even be promoted into higher positions."

"We defund Kalinka. They have no money, they have no moles," Emil said. I heard Janina grimace in pain through the receiver as I slipped another coin into the slot of the payphone.

"Do you think this is the start of a coup, Janina?" I asked.

"If it is, we need to act quickly. Defund them, like Emil said. Their energy contracts are the most valuable things they hold. Since Putin left office, Medvedev has been like some estranged cousin to Kalinka and refuses to fund the group directly. He's trying to maintain a cleaner public image than Putin had as Russian president. Putin was sympathetic to Kalinka since, as a former KGB officer, he had many friends in their circle. Medvedev is more mild. Still controlled by Putin, but less belligerent on the global stage. Medvedev won't fund them, so Kalinka has set up valuable energy contracts across the Baltic region to generate income."

"Do they have offices? How do we get to their banking information?" I asked.

"Slow down. Getting their cash is one problem, the other is destroying the nuclear reactor."

"I was worried she was going to suggest that," Emil whispered, turning away from the payphone.

"You'll need a nuclear scientist for that one. A good one. Disarm the computer, remove the nuclear rods, and shut the whole thing down, tunnel and all." Janina's voice had become even weaker. "I have to go."

"Tell us how to get to the money," I attempted one more time to ask for advice in getting anything that could lead us to their bank account.

"Start at the tunnel. That's all I know." The audio from Janina's phone became staticky, as if it were rubbing against her clothes or the bed sheets. I overheard the voices of hospital personnel entering her room asking if she was alright and then hung up the payphone.

With a deep breath, I started across the square towards Hotel La Pologne, Emil trailing a few steps behind me.

"We probably shouldn't go back," Emil said as he jogged to catch up to me. He nodded up at the second-floor terrace door of our hotel room. I had left it open to air out the room, but now saw the figures of two men dressed in dark clothes walking around inside.

"That doesn't look like room service," I responded. I pulled out my phone to search for another hotel nearby.

17

Emil and I, again, abandoned our belongings at Hotel La Pologne and relocated to a bed-and-breakfast on the outskirts of Warsaw. We arrived at the small standalone home, owned by an older woman. I shouldn't have been shocked to discover that she not only owned the bed-and-breakfast, but also did the cooking, cleaning, and entertaining of guests. She could have been one hundred years old, but she seemed just as youthful as us. She would most likely run the place until she died.

We had left the Alfa Romeo in an empty parking lot in the opposite direction of our new accommodations, knowing that Marek, if he was affiliated with Kalinka, would be looking for us. Or, at the very least, I guessed that my cousin would demand that her husband hunt down her new car, wherever it might have been in Warsaw.

We were starting over again and needed new clothes, new cosmetics, and a new vehicle, but instead, we were focused on Janina's words. If it was true that we needed a scientist to disarm the nuclear reactor in the tunnel, we only had one option, and we were determined to exercise it.

Golecki's neurotic behavior suggested he might also be a workaholic, so we drove to the SKW offices once again to see if we could pick him up. It was understood that he might be hesitant, or even unwilling, to help, but we had no other choice.

The receptionist didn't work on Saturdays, leaving the security guard to be the only remaining obstacle between us and entrance into the SKW. I walked into the atrium where we had been the day before for our debriefs with Jaworski. I was alone and the building was silent. From around the corner, the security guard who had scanned us on Tuesday evening and Friday morning appeared.

"Miss Sosna, is it?" He asked, recognizing me immediately. "The offices of the SKW are formally closed on weekends and especially today, in light of the morning's events in Smoleńsk.

We've closed our offices so agents can pay respects and grieve at home."

"I completely understand, Officer…"

"Taleta."

"Officer Taleta. My intent wasn't to see Skiba or Jaworski today. Actually," I fluttered my eyelashes and looked up at the tall, uniformed man. "I came to see you."

"Oh." The officer seemed dumbfounded. He wasn't particularly attractive, not like Emil, and I guessed that he probably felt quite flattered. I stepped forward to bring myself closer to him.

"You know, you really helped us this week with your insistence that we see an SKW director on Tuesday," I started saying slowly. The officer's back was now turned to the front doors. Just then, I saw Emil peek through the small window at the entrance and, seeing that the officer's back was to him, he quietly pulled the door open.

"It was nothing, ma'am– "

"No, really, Officer Taleta. I'm sure you heard we are only in town for a few days, so your help in getting us a meeting was priceless. It made a big difference in the task we were trying to accomplish…" I ran my hand down his left arm, then took his hand into mine and pulled him closer to me. "I just wanted to come back and express my gratitude."

Emil snuck around the corner of the atrium and entered the emergency stairway, slipping out of sight. His access was just one part of the errand at the SKW. The next was keeping the officer busy enough to neglect his duties and allow enough time for Emil to come back down with Golecki.

I started kissing the officer gently, then allowed him to kiss back more intensely.

"Is there… a room we could use?" I asked politely, feigning decency. He smiled crookedly at me, clearly elated beyond words, and then took me down a hallway, turning into a janitor's closet, which smelled putridly of bleach. We spent all of 10 minutes in the tightly enclosed space before my phone vibrated in my pocket, giving me the signal that I could come back to the car. I pushed the officer away gently and faked a smile.

"Here's my number," I jotted down a false set of digits onto a notepad I pulled out of my purse and handed it to him. "Give me a call when you're off duty. We'll pick up where we left off, I hope."

I readjusted my clothes, smoothed my hair back, then opened the door of the closet and walked down the hallway. Before I left the building, I turned to blow a kiss to the trailing officer. He was clueless.

~ ~ ~

I got into the back of the newly rented midsize Volvo, relieved to see Golecki in the front passenger seat of the car. The car was already started, ready for the trip back north.

"You could have fucking called me first," Golecki said to me, annoyed, as I buckled into my seat. I couldn't help but smile at his paranoia. Emil promptly put the car into gear and sped onto the road. "This guy scared the shit out of me sneaking into my office. And you're lucky it's a weekend because if it had been a weekday, I would have been kicking and screaming on my way out of the SKW. I have too much work to do, especially on a day like today."

"But you're coming with us voluntarily now? Of your own free will?" Emil asked. Golecki rolled his eyes, ceding his stance, and moved onto the next subject, which was laying out the plan for penetrating the tunnel that night.

We spent most of the drive recounting our conversation with Janina, attempting to relay every detail she discussed with us to Golecki. He listened carefully and asked meticulous questions. It was refreshing to speak to someone else who was informed about Kalinka and the tunnel and, for the first time since meeting Magda and Janina, to know that this person was not suspicious. He couldn't be. Even though he was apparently a brilliant scientist, he was too young to have risen in the ranks of SKW in his short career. The ladder was crowded at the top, as Golecki put it, and if he wanted to get promoted any further, he essentially needed to wait until the corrupt generation before him, the one that was established when communism fell, died out.

"So why are you making pennies at the SKW when a tech company could be paying you millions?" I asked once we had finished discussing the plans for the tunnel. We were about an hour from the tripoint. "You could be working in London or Silicon Valley or any other hub in the world. I'd bet you could even name your price."

"It's something I've always wanted to do, I suppose," he said with a hint of embarrassment. "This government thing, I mean. And it's something I've felt I should do. It's not about money for me. Can we stop for a coffee or something?"

Golecki's confidence was like that of an adolescent. If I had a younger brother, I felt like Golecki would resemble him in his uncertainty. He was prepared to take away the nuclear power of a post-KGB mafia-like political organization, but he couldn't hold a conversation with two adults his own age.

I hoped his cleverness would outweigh his self-doubt at the tripoint.

18

"I brought my gun from my desk, but what do you have for arms?" Golecki asked as we neared the tripoint, passing familiar landscapes and road signs that Emil and I had seen earlier that week.

"Walthers," Emil responded.

"That's it? You've got to be kidding me."

"We have ammo in the back," I added, hoping it would relieve some of Golecki's anxiety.

"You're trying to take down Kalinka and you're driving up here without semi-automatics? Detonators? Body armor?" Golecki rubbed his forehead. "You two are going to give me a stroke today."

Just after 7:00 that evening, we pulled into the parking lot across the street from Café Gadam. The church, gas station, and restaurant on that intersection were just as quiet as they had been on

Tuesday. Visibility was worse because the sun had already set, and the roads were poorly lit. Only the excess light falling through the windows of the gas station and restaurant dimly illuminated the intersection.

We entered Café Gadam, but the main seating area of the restaurant was completely empty. There were no diners at the tables, no wait staff washing dishes, and no guests at the bar. Soft Slavic folk music played over the speakers, but no one greeted us. Emil, Golecki, and I were all armed, our guns tucked into our belts underneath our coats, but there wasn't a reason to use them yet. I wondered if they had already vacated Café Gadam and removed all evidence of their activity from the tunnel. There was only one way to find out.

"They've either left, or they're waiting for us," Emil said. "Otherwise, we'd be dead already."

He walked towards the circular area rug and kicked it aside, revealing a latch door in the floorboards. There was a fastening that I imagined would normally hold a lock, but there was nothing securing the door to the floor. Emil looked at me.

"Pull it open," I said, finally taking out my gun. I pointed it towards the floor as Emil threw the latch door back, exposing a square hole beneath it. At the edge of the opening rested the top of a ladder, which led down a shaft about five or six meters to the ground floor of the tunnel.

Golecki, resourcefully, had a flashlight in his pocket and shined it down the hole so we could each descend. When we got to the bottom of the hole, we turned around from the ladder and looked down a long, cement-reinforced, dark path ahead of us.

I let Emil and Golecki walk ahead of me as I recollected in my mind the history written into the walls of this extensive passage. I envisioned my grandfather first breaking ground here, with Magda and the rest of his platoon, just months after the end of the war, already willing to make sacrifices again. I imagined the innocent platoon being massacred at the Lithuanian end of the tunnel, with just Dziadek and Magda left as the lone survivors, commanded to bury their countrymen in the forest, without any dignity. And then I pictured Magda, an enslaved woman who served the Soviets and then Kalinka for her entire adult life in this tunnel. She lived and died a slave, even if Poland was considered a free country. She never even tasted the air of liberation.

"Joanna," Emil called ahead of me, bringing my attention back to our planned approach.

"Coming."

There was a light on the right side of the tunnel a few hundred meters ahead of us. As we stepped closer to the light, which slipped into the dark tunnel through a crack in a door, I started hearing light murmurs. It sounded like three or four people and I picked up at least one hushed woman's voice.

We arrived at the door, our guns drawn ahead of us. My heart beat loudly while I prayed a Hail Mary in my head, as I told Wujek in the church I sometimes did.

...Pray for us sinners now, and at the hour of our death.

I nodded at Emil to open the door, which he tapped gently with his foot. The creaking wooden door swung open and, before we could see the room inside, we heard the voices fall silent and the cocking sound of loaded guns at the ready.

The door opened completely, and we remained in the entryway facing three armed men, whom I recognized from Tuesday's encounter at Café Gadam, and a woman sitting in a leather chair behind a desk. I scanned the faces of all four individuals in the room, but my eyes remained on the woman. She was maybe 60 years old, but made obvious attempts to look younger, so she might have passed for 50. She boasted a flattering body-contouring black dress with three-quarter sleeves and a boat neck, potentially purchased from the Chanel Spring/Summer 2009 collection; I knew the dress because I had seen it myself on a runway in Paris during fashion week. Beneath the desk, I could see she wore polished, black stiletto heels. Her eyes were heavily made up and, had I not considered treatment for myself in the past, I would have missed the slightest trace of Botox injections around her mouth and along her cheekbones that smoothed out her face. She was stunning for her age while clinging to the beauty she had enjoyed in her youth.

It wasn't her impressive outfit or physique that kept my eyes on her, but her face. When I glanced at Emil in the entryway and his eyes met mine, I knew he saw it, too. The resemblance was unmistakable.

If you stripped away the lavish clothing and added 20 pounds, she was indistinguishable in appearance from Janina.

"Welcome, welcome, welcome," the woman said in a thick Eastern European accent. If she hadn't been surrounded by three enormous Russian men holding guns in our direction, I would have misinterpreted her voice and greeting as warm and hospitable. "I've been looking forward to this meeting for the past few days. What an eventful week we've had, Miss Sosna!"

I looked in Emil's direction again, and then at Golecki, to see if either of them recognized who we were speaking to. It was as if she were receiving an old friend, not an antagonist from halfway across the world. We entered the room through the open door, our guns still drawn.

"Let's all play nice, darlings, and put our toys away. Let's not let our shiny guns distract us from a pleasant conversation," the woman said. The three men on her side of the room uncocked their pistols and lowered them to their sides. Once we knew they weren't bluffing, we did the same, releasing the tiniest bit of tension in the room.

"Who are you?" I asked.

"I'm the one you've all been dying, quite literally, to see," she replied with a sinister smile on her face. "I am Kalinka."

"*You're* Kalinka?" Emil clarified, aghast. She nodded slowly, still smiling. The SKW impressed upon us that Kalinka was the name of the entire organization and that it was named either after the Kaliningrad Oblast or as a nickname using the first letter of the Soviet acronym KGB. The woman before us was now transforming our understanding of the agency. We had the embodiment of Kalinka in front of our own eyes.

"You've waited for us. Why?" I asked.

"Well, I requested that you return home earlier today, and I figured if you weren't on the last plane out of Warsaw to Chicago by the end of the day, the only other place you would be was right here in this tunnel that you so cleverly discovered earlier this week," Kalinka responded. She stood up from her seat and walked gracefully around to the front of her desk, leaning against it and crossing her arms delicately over her chest. "Tell me, how did you find it? My friend Kacper didn't live to hear, but I'd love to know. Was it a secret note? Did your Dziadek tell you in confidence on his deathbed?"

"Coordinates, actually," Emil said. "Encrypted in his war memoir, the key being a letter read at his funeral."

"Oh! The funeral that Kacper was at? That little dolt should have picked up on that. But enough about the past. He got what he deserved at the end of the day. And, Yury, correct me if I'm wrong, but we recouped every penny of the 20,000 dollars we promised him, right?"

"*Da*," the man towering over her to her right confirmed in Russian.

"He wasn't worth it," Kalinka snickered softly and shook her head, covering her mouth with her hand. She seemed a bit delusional, or like she had taken a stimulant drug immediately before our arrival, but I made sure I didn't sell her short for her peculiar behavior.

"We aren't going home," I responded.

"Well, then, I consider this meeting a formal going away party for you to change your mind. I know you love Poland. God, Country, Honor. It's all so sentimentally patriotic. I love patriotism!" Kalinka exclaimed. She was obviously enjoying the dialogue. "But Poland is taking a little bit of a turn in history right now, as you read in the newspaper this morning. And, I'm sorry to say, but you will have no part in it. You will go home tomorrow, back to America. Your citizenship will be revoked by the time the government turns over. You'll be, like your grandfathers were, Damned Soldiers, no? You come back into this country and you'll be killed."

I noticed Golecki gazing around the room, observing the ceiling and the walls of the office. I could hardly tell we were underground with how nicely the room had been built.

"Forgive my scientific curiosity, Miss Kalinka, but I have to ask. How has this tunnel been maintained for so long?" He began pacing around the back of the room, past a line of wooden floor cabinets on which sat stacks of papers.

"Oh, I am so happy you asked! We don't get a lot of visitors, and the ones we do see don't live very long," Kalinka said, giggling to herself again. "As you know, Sosna and his platoon started this project in 1945 after the end of the war. The Soviets came about two years later and borrowed the tunnel, removing all but two people of the platoon. One being Sosna, the other being Magda. Oh, forgive my digression, but I'm not sure if you heard. Your cousin's husband did end up killing Magda and her daughter."

"We're aware," I responded, withdrawing any emotion from my voice.

"Oh, good. So we're all caught up. Anyway, Sosna escaped to the States, that little rascal, and Magda ended up working for us for the past 60 years. She did such a wonderful job, that old woman, never told a soul about the tunnel. She was so trustworthy, we couldn't bear to let her go. I'll miss her, I think. She was so obedient." Kalinka walked over to a mini bar in the corner of the office, pulled out a clear bottle of vodka from the freezer underneath it, and began pouring glasses for each of us.

"The infrastructure, Miss Kalinka," Golecki prompted, still walking near the cabinets and staring at the ceiling.

"Ah, yes. I do apologize, I just enjoy your presence so much. The tunnel was excavated in a very rudimentary manner, so, yes, we needed to reinforce it when the Soviets took over. The entire tunnel was originally much more narrow and, when we found it, it was propped up with wooden planks. We had a team of miners and civil engineers come from the Soviet Union immediately to inspect the soil conditions and the surrounding elements that could impact the integrity of the tunnel, and they recommended rock bolts, I believe, which were relatively easy to install, as well as one of the first forms of shotcrete. It wasn't that extraordinary, darling, it was just securing what had already been made. Tunnels have been manmade since the times of the Romans, you know."

Golecki continued to make his way around the back of the room, running his hands over any exposed shotcrete, his back to us. I rolled my eyes at his obliviousness to his own idiosyncrasies. He wasn't helping us by drawing attention to his "scientific curiosities" in that moment.

"So, shall we drink to your departure and safe return to the States?" Kalinka asked, bringing glasses of vodka to each of us. "Because, darlings, I really don't want to have to terminate you like I had to do with Kacper. I am not that kind of person all the time, I want you to just go back quietly to your nice life, as if this never happened. You'll see events unravel on the television, but you'll know you were saved from any kind of turmoil. In short, I'm giving you a way out."

"Yes!" Golecki exclaimed suddenly, turning abruptly from his investigation of the walls. Emil and I tried to mask our shock, not only at his enthusiasm, but also at his willingness to drink. I wanted to remind him that vodka didn't have caffeine, but before I could finish thinking through the line in my head, he took a glass abrasively from Kalinka's hand and drank its entire contents in one swig. All of us, even Kalinka, stared at him in disbelief.

"Goodness, boy, has no one ever taught you how to drink with company?" Kalinka asked, perhaps the most appalled of us all.

"I don't have friends. Don't need them," Golecki responded, then turned back around. "We should probably be going. I think Joanna and Emil understand what is expected of them."

Golecki walked to the entryway and exited into the tunnel.

"Excellent!" Kalinka proclaimed. It was like she had won the lottery. "I have contacts at the airport, so I'll check in with them tomorrow to make sure you're on that last flight to Chicago. Don't be late!"

Emil and I followed Golecki's lead and walked towards the tunnel.

"One more question, Miss Kalinka," Golecki said before we left completely.

"Yes, little scientist man?" I looked at Golecki to see his reaction, but he didn't flinch at the beratement. He was probably used to it and was either too socially inept or too apathetic to care.

"Aren't you concerned for me saying anything about this tunnel to anyone?" He asked, leaning into the room.

"Oh, the most difficult part of our drama has already unfolded this morning. The rest of the pieces will fall right into place. Everyone will be doing as I command and anyone currently working for the government will just be working for the new one, once it is established. Besides, you are too far down the totem pole to raise any red flags or blow any whistles. And even if red flags were raised, it's too late to do anything about a coup now," Kalinka explained calmly, the same professional smile still on her face.

"Right," Golecki responded, and then turned back around to the tunnel, exiting up the ladder to Café Gadam with us.

"What the hell was all of that?" Emil whispered as soon as we were outside. We rushed into the Volvo, started the car, and sped off south.

"Go back to Warsaw," Golecki said. "You're getting on a plane tomorrow."

"To Chicago?" I asked.

"No, to Zurich." Golecki pulled open his unzipped jacket and unbuttoned his shirt to his sternum. He revealed a small camera taped to his chest.

"Golecki, you're brilliant," I said.

"I didn't know if it would come in handy, but I thought I'd wear one in case I needed to memorize anything extensive. The papers in the back were bank statements. I have the bank account number recorded."

"So we fly to her bank in Switzerland tomorrow and do what? Casually withdraw the balance of the account, without so much as a password?" Emil asked, driving down the dark road, dozens of kilometers above the speed limit.

"We don't have her password, but we have the next best thing," I said from the back seat of the car.

"What's that?" Golecki asked.

"Kalinka's identical twin sister," Emil responded, his eyes on the road. "We have to go to Suwałki tonight to pick her up."

"Wait, how the hell do you know Kalinka's twin sister?" Golecki was astounded, turning frantically from Emil to me, then back again.

"Magda's daughter, Janina, is Kalinka's twin," I explained.

"You're sure?" Golecki asked.

"Positive," Emil confirmed.

"And Marek didn't pick up on this when he was at her house? He didn't draw the connection between the twins?" Golecki clarified.

"Kalinka keeps a tightly knit circle. He's probably never even met Kalinka, kind of like our friend Kacper in Chicago. Her entourage makes all the arrangements, pays all the compensation, and pulls the trigger whenever someone needs to be taken out. She keeps her hands clean," Emil explained. It made sense.

"I've worked with banks in Switzerland in the past," I turned our attention back to the bank. "We have a few accounts overseas. I know their security restrictions and how we can gain access to accounts, especially higher value accounts with stricter controls."

"Like what?" Emil asked.

"They have sophisticated methods of identification. Passwords are a thing of the past. They're not secure enough and can get into the wrong hands. Banks do a DNA match now to access accounts."

"So, if that's the case, then if we have Janina, we essentially have Kalinka," Emil said.

"Not exactly," Golecki objected. "Only about 10 percent of identical twins carry identical DNA. There are often genetic mutations between twins, even if they were conceived of the same sperm and egg."

"Then we take the risk. We don't have another choice," I decided. I felt much less confident than I sounded about a potential blood test.

"Emil?" I asked after a few minutes of silence. Another concern, this time about my family's history, crossed my mind.

"Yeah?"

"Did you draw the same conclusion about Magda and her daughters as I did?" Emil took a moment to respond, knowing what his answer might imply about my grandfather and his faithfulness after the war. He worked on the tunnel for at least a year with Magda before he was reunited with my grandmother and left Poland.

"Yes." My stomach dropped at our mutual presumption.

"Do you think he ever knew that Magda got pregnant?"

"Hold on a second," Golecki interrupted. He was catching up to the conversation and the gaps in knowledge that Emil and I were filling in by ourselves. "Are you saying that Janina and Kalinka are– "

"My father's half-sisters," I finished his sentence, leaving no room for doubt. I stared out the window at the passing trees, the distant image of what I knew to be my family, now deceased, locked in my mind. I was just now realizing that the picture of our family had been incomplete. He never told his wife, he never told my father, and he never told me.

"*Ja pierdole,*" Golecki cursed. He was right, we were capable of causing a stroke in him that night. "And Janina has no idea she has a twin sister?"

"None," I responded.

"How were they split up? How did Janina remain with Magda and Kalinka end up with the Soviets?" Emil asked the question I was still trying to resolve in my own mind.

"Magda kept saying that they were blackmailing her," I said. "This is terrible, but I think they took Kalinka from her after they were born. They held her baby over her head and told her to work for them or she'd never seen Kalinka again. And then they raised the child themselves."

"Poor Magda..." Emil whispered. "One of her daughters took care of her for the rest of her life, the other one imprisoned her. Kalinka probably rose in the ranks of the organization and then led it."

"Magda couldn't even tell Kalinka she was her mother. They'd kill all of them if she did," I said. "She protected them both."

We remained quiet for the rest of the car ride until we arrived at the hospital where Janina was staying. We had been lucky this entire trip with chance encounters and fortunate conversations leading us from one place to another. The next test was whether Janina was strong enough, and willing enough, to learn the truth about her past and join us in Switzerland.

19

When we arrived at the hospital, we were able to find Janina without an issue. Once again, it seemed like none of the nursing staff cared about patient privacy. I was astounded at the lack of medical discretion but welcomed the loophole.

The three of us entered Janina's room quietly and, realizing she was sleeping, sat down on the chairs near the door. As Golecki passed us to sit in the third empty chair, he kicked the metal medical cart, sending it rolling loudly across the white tile floor, its pills and utensils clattering on the top tray. Emil groaned at his clumsiness as Janina blinked awake, looking at her three new visitors.

"You made it to the tunnel?" She asked weakly, propping herself up in her bed. She adjusted the recline with the remote attached to the rail and tucked her frizzy hair behind her ear.

"We did. And we found Kalinka," I said.

"How many of them are there?" Janina inquired, smoothing the sheets on her bed across her lap. "How many do we need to take down?"

"Janina, Kalinka isn't the name of the organization… It's the name of a woman," Emil explained slowly.

"What was she like?"

"She was about your age, your height," I started carefully. "She had your eyes, your lips, your entire face. We think Kalinka is your twin."

Janina stared blankly at us and, after a moment of silence, Golecki started fidgeting loudly in his pocket, pulling out his phone, the disconnected body camera, and a cord.

"I took a video…" He began as he set up his devices to demonstrate Kalinka to Janina. After a minute of navigating across different screens on his phone, he finally played the video recording saved to the body camera. He fast-forwarded the replay to the moment we walked through the door, and he paused the video on the first clear view we could see of Kalinka behind her desk.

Janina took the phone into her hands and spent several minutes pressing play and pause through the recording, her eyes scanning the screen.

"It does look like me," she finally said, setting the phone down on her bed. There was a sadness and a resign in her voice. None of us wanted to believe that the woman who had enslaved her own mother, and then commanded her death, was Janina's own blood sister. "Though I wish I looked that young and thin."

"Janina, you said at your house on Tuesday that your mother was in the resistance," I spoke again. "We think your father was, too."

"I never knew my father."

Emil, Golecki, and I exchanged glances. I stood up from my chair and walked to the side of her bed, taking her hand. I crouched closer to the floor, so our faces were at the same level, and looked into her eyes.

"We think your father was my Dziadek."

Janina blinked at me. I imagined she was calculating her age, envisioning the end of the war, reconstructing Magda and Henryk's work on the tunnel, and remembering the coincidence that they were the only two survivors after the Soviets discovered it. When it clicked in her mind that she believed my statement was true, she took a deep, shaky breath. Tears flooded her eyes.

"Your father was my half-brother," she declared. "So you are my niece."

My eyes stung with tears at the sound of the word *niece*. For my entire life, I never had an extended family. It was always my parents and my grandparents, plus any distant relatives, like Agata, that lived in Poland. I had now unearthed a new side of my past, my existence. It was complicated and troubling, but at the same time comforting. Janina was my aunt.

"Janina, we need to ask you to do something for us," I continued, wiping my eyes with the back of my sleeve.

"Yes," she was paying attention, wiping her tears with a tissue she found in the folds of her bedding. She propped herself up again.

"Kalinka doesn't know she has a twin. She expects that we will be leaving the country tomorrow, so we need to move quickly before she realizes what we are up to. We came here because we need your help. Kalinka's has Swiss bank accounts that are secured by a sophisticated system of DNA identification. We think you and Kalinka may share the same genetic makeup. If we want to defund the organization, we need you to come to Zurich with us tomorrow," I explained, rising from the floor and returning to my seat.

"I'll be weak, but I can do it."

"We'll need to dress you like Kalinka. You'll need to act a little differently, speak a little differently… The bankers she works with have seen her personally and have a certain expectation of how she would behave," Emil added. Janina nodded quickly and waved her hand, as if she already knew what was being expected of her.

"Alright. Get a doctor in here. We move tonight."

Janina was discharged from the hospital an hour later after a final exam and enough bandaging to last her another day. She scheduled a follow-up appointment for Monday with the same doctor and left the building, limping, with us.

Her home was just a 20-minute drive from the hospital. When we arrived, she commanded us around her house, telling me what to pack, Emil where to find her passport, and Golecki to water her orchids on the windowsill. We all quickly obliged, booked our flights to Zurich over the phone, then headed to Warsaw for the night.

~ ~ ~

My phone rang in the car that night as we neared Warsaw. I checked the caller ID and announced to Emil that Agata was calling me again.

"If Agata's working with Marek and Kalinka, they'd be able to track you down anyway," Emil advised. "Take the call."

"Hello?" I answered the phone. Before I heard a response, there were sniffles and soft sobs on the other end of the line.

"Joanna," Agata said. There was a definite, unconcealed misery in her voice.

"Agata, what's wrong?" I asked my cousin. I expected her snarky, energetic voice, but instead received bereavement.

"Marek hasn't come home for a few days. He's not answering his cell phone. He hasn't been this unresponsive, not since he left his old job at the SKW," Agata responded quietly. "It's like he's working in the field again. Do you know where he is?"

My heart sank as I jumped to the conclusion that Kalinka, after commanding Marek to kill Magda and whomever he found at her house, had found out that he hadn't completed his entire assignment. I assumed Kalinka had reprimanded him by taking his life.

"I don't, Agata. I'm sorry." I didn't ask questions and didn't ask how I could help her.

"When are you coming back to Warsaw? Did everything go alright at the tripoint?" She asked sadly, concerned for my wellbeing.

"Things are still… in process. We might be going back to Chicago soon." I was careful not to divulge any more details than necessary. If Marek had betrayed us, there was a chance that Agata was involved with Kalinka, too. Women could so easily emotionally manipulate others. I presumed, for my own safety, that this was an act to lure me back into Kalinka's control.

"But you just got to Poland. Stay with me in Warsaw, please, at least until Marek gets back," Agata begged. I resisted the urge to comfort her, tell her everything that had taken place, and let her know that her husband was conspiring against the government.

"Not tonight, Agata. I'm sorry. Emil and I have some things we need to discuss," I said, giving a reason for our absence.

"Your texts to me earlier were so cryptic!" Agata said, her tone suddenly changing from sullen to inquisitive. "Are you sleeping with him?"

"Agata– "

"You don't have to be explicit about details, you can just say 'yes' or 'no' if he is in the same room as you," she said lightheartedly despite the sniffles.

"It's complicated. I'll tell you everything over brunch when I'm free one of these days, deal?" I asked. I hoped my offer would satiate her thirst for sensational information on my love life.

"Deal. Stay safe, cousin," she said, and then hung up the phone.

"How is she?" Emil asked immediately.

"Marek hasn't come home. I think Kalinka took him out, knowing he didn't finish off Janina," I responded, putting my phone into my pocket again.

"Kalinka knows about me?" Janina asked, a tinge of worry in her voice.

"She knows Magda has a daughter," I said, facing the passenger window again. "She has no idea that daughter is her twin."

20

Emil convinced us to book two separate flights. I would go first to Zurich with Janina, and he would come on the next flight an hour later with Golecki. Emil had good reason to suggest the divided approach; if Kalinka could take down one plane, she could take down another.

On our flight to Zurich, I trained Janina on her own sister's mannerisms. I had chosen a few outfits from Janina's fancier side of her closet, dresses reserved for banquets, church, and weddings, and packed them the night before. I explained to her how she should change her behavior and language when speaking to the bankers.

"You have to be overly excited, but also professional. Kalinka is smart, so use flowery but intelligent words," I said, sipping the cappuccino I had purchased earlier near our departure gate.

"I haven't practiced my English in a few years…"

"That's fine. Remember, I am posing as your daughter to whom you are entrusting the balance of the account and leadership of the organization. I will be there supporting you through the dialogue."

"And if they ask me a question and I don't know how to respond?" She asked. Every time Janina spoke, she seemed more nervous.

"One of us will respond on your behalf. Remember, I'm your daughter, Emil is my fiancé, and Golecki is our financial advisor."

"Golecki's a scientist," Janina contended.

"But a brilliant one, and his knowledge of SKW cases in financial crimes is extensive. He knows how to talk money," I responded confidently. The more I could demonstrate my own self-certainty, the more I hoped I could boost hers.

"Alright."

"How's your torso? Are you able to walk straight later today? Emil called Zurich Swiss One this morning and let them know Kalinka wanted to arrange a meeting, so we are set for noon."

"On a Sunday?"

"I think if the Pope wanted to meet with the bankers at the same time as Kalinka, they would choose her over him. Oh, and one more thing," I added. "Kalinka has contacts at Chopin International and they've been directed to keep an eye out for our names. They'll know Emil and I are on a flight to Zurich, not a flight that flies directly to Chicago, so she will be on the hunt for us."

"In Switzerland or in Poland?" Janina asked.

"Wherever they can catch us."

Janina seemed flustered. She shuffled through her purse and pulled out a three-ounce plastic bottle of Smirnoff vodka, unscrewed the cap, and poured its contents into the cup of orange juice on the tray table in front of her. She took a few sips from the cup, then turned back to me.

"If I die by liquidating millions from the bitch who held my mother hostage for her entire life, it would be the best way to go."

~ ~ ~

Before heading to the headquarters of Zurich Swiss One, Janina and I made a detour to pick up a few remaining items to complete her attire for the meeting with the bankers. We stopped at a boutique for high enough black heels and then an atelier for a blazer she could wear over her dress. Emil and Golecki met us at the atelier shortly after we arrived. We hadn't even waited on them since we filled our time with shopping.

After we purchased the blazer at the atelier, I huddled into a changing room with Janina while Emil browsed premade suits and Golecki inspected neckties as if he had never seen them before. By the time we emerged, I had transformed Janina, by all accounts of physical attributes, into her sister. She walked out with the same poise and tenacity as Kalinka, controlling the room with a single, deadly look.

"You've created a monster," Golecki blurted from across the sitting area of the atelier.

"No," I demurred. "I've created *the* monster."

I had replicated Kalinka's make up onto Janina's face. The smoky eye shadow, lash extensions, and plum lipstick did make her look like a villain. I got goosebumps at the sight of my recreation. It was like a three-dimensional printer had just delivered a live copy of the very woman from whom we were about to embezzle millions of euros.

We took a cab to Zurich Swiss One and signed in at the reception, receiving name tags that each of us pinned to our chests. We were greeted promptly by a man who seemed to be about Janina's age. The lobby was quiet on that weekend afternoon and his voice echoed across the chic concrete floors.

"Miss Kalinka!" He announced cheerfully, smiling as he walked regally with open arms towards Janina. He was practically singing with joy. It was like he was receiving his own beloved mother.

"Darling!" Janina responded in her accent, which was just as thick as Kalinka's. I held my breath on this first encounter to see if her appearance and mannerisms were believable. The banker embraced Janina and gave her an extravagant kiss on each cheek.

"My God, it's been years since you've been here!" He exclaimed, his hands covering his mouth. "Turn around, let me see you in those Manolo Blahniks."

Janina obliged like a puppet, a bashful smile on her face.

"Now stop, you're making me blush," Janina said. She was in perfect character. I couldn't have envisioned a better portrayal of her sister.

"This must be your daughter, is that right? Miss Sosna?" The banker took my hand and, bowing, kissed the top of it.

"You can call me Joanna," I responded. "And this is my fiancé, Emil. And our financial advisor, he's just here to ride along for the fun."

"Excellent! Let's go up to the board room, we'll chat more there."

We followed the banker into an elevator and rode it up to the fifth floor. We still did not know what we should call him. We assumed that Kalinka would know not only his full name, but the breed of his dog, his partner's name, his home address, and his favorite restaurant in Zurich. He needn't introduce himself to her, but we instructed Janina to use the filler word "darling" in case of any direct reference to him.

"Here we are," the banker stepped out of the elevator, holding the door open with his hand, and allowed us to exit after him.

"My, my, this place has changed, hasn't it?" Janina said, making an effort to initiate small talk after some silence.

"Well, yes, I suppose you could say that. We moved buildings after our lease ran out in the old one on Bahnhofstrasse, which is where you would have last visited us."

"That would explain it! God, it's been years," Janina exclaimed.

We entered a wood-paneled board room in which a large screen was set up with a Zurich Swiss One-branded greeting that displayed the words *Welcome Chereshenko Family!* Another piece of the puzzle had been serendipitously found – Kalinka's surname.

"Now, let's get down to business, as I understand your return flight is this evening, yes?" The banker said, sitting down in a chair and pulling his leatherbound portfolio across the table toward him. We all sat down next to the banker, Janina and I closest to him, then Emil and Golecki furthest from him. In the bottom righthand side of the cover of his portfolio, his name, Daniel Keller, was embellished in gold font.

"That's right, Mr. Keller," I responded.

"Please. Daniel!" He corrected me, opening his portfolio and placing his hand on my wrist. I faked embarrassment to show him I was flattered that we were on a first name basis already. "Now, I didn't even know you had a daughter before today. You never spoke of her, and she wasn't even a beneficiary on any of your accounts."

"I wanted to keep her out of the business. You know, the work can get... complicated sometimes. It's best to keep loved ones out of it, especially your own children," Janina answered flawlessly.

"I understand, of course. I am elated to be meeting her now. And what's the task we'd like to accomplish today? You're here in person, so I have to assume we're talking about cash?"

"That's right," Janina said, clearing her throat. "I am retiring from the organization after so many years of devoted work. I'll be transferring the balance of my account to Joanna and her fiancé so they can endeavor fruitfully into their new life together and take over leadership. Two young heads are better than my old one, you know."

"Ah, yes. The organization seems to be reaching a pivotal moment, is it not? I was listening to the news yesterday and heard about the plane crash. Jarring, isn't it? And then I saw snippets of what looks to be a coup at the Chancellery building. Just chaos, but it's the fruit of your labor. How does that saying go... One man's trash is another man's treasure?"

"I think the phrase is 'one man's terrorist is another man's freedom fighter,'" Golecki piped up from the outskirts of the boardroom table. I sent him a menacing glare.

"Brilliant! Illustrious!" Daniel laughed. "Well, my congratulations to you, Joanna and Emil, on your engagement. I am sure everything will be left in trustful hands. And congratulations to you, Kalinka, on your early retirement. Now, which account are we going to be transferring from?" This question we had not considered. Before I could think of a response, Janina spoke.

"You know the one..." She said, looking slyly at Daniel across the table. If she hadn't been speaking of money or to an obviously homosexual man, I'd think she was flirting.

"Oh, the large one? That's quite the balance we're going to be moving," Daniel responded, flipping through some pages that were filed in his portfolio.

"Can you remind me the balance in it?" Janina asked, leaning forward curiously.

"We are currently at about 570 million euros in the liquid cash account."

My stomach dropped. I hadn't anticipated the size of the balance, as money had never been an issue for me with my inheritance. I was never in need of it. The balance in this account was comparable to the reserves of a small country.

"Yes, that'll be all of it," Janina confirmed.

"And the rest of the investment accounts?" Daniel asked.

"Balances?"

"They're tiny. A million, here or there, in each of the five accounts. Truthfully, we should have consolidated ages ago, but time flies and little pennies like this sometimes go unnoticed," Daniel explained, erupting into laughter. Golecki laughed across the table with him in the same ostentatious manner, which caused Emil to crack a smile as well.

"Well, there's no time like the present. Let's consolidate it all into the cash account, sell the investments, and transfer everything," Janina said.

"Any concerns on the capital gains? Perhaps tax questions on your ongoing operations with the organizations?" Daniel's eyes scanned the room.

"Do we look like we'd be concerned about taxes?" I asked mischievously, which caused Daniel to laugh again.

"Oh, she's rich, darling. Just rich... And what will be left for you, Kalinka?" Daniel asked with a worried tone. "Are you cheating banks with us and keeping cash in some other tax haven that we don't know about?" The second question was asked more playfully.

"Darling, you know I would never choose anyone other than Zurich Swiss One. The truth is…" Janina paused and looked over at me, her theatrical demeanor changing to sad.

"The truth is that Mother was just diagnosed with early stages of Alzheimer's," I finished her sentence. "It's very aggressive, and she has been forgetting important appointments, events, even people. No wonder she forgot that the bank moved offices."

"And so you're retiring… My great condolences, Kalinka," Daniel said. At that moment, Janina pulled out a tissue from her Yves Saint Laurent purse and dabbed at the inside corners of her eyes. Daniel looked as if he might cry, too.

"Thank you, darling. You're a true friend."

"Now, Joanna, will you be holding an account with our bank, or a different one?" Daniel asked, clearing his throat.

"We will actually be going through Credit Suisse. I have existing relationships there, and we'd like to maintain them, if you don't mind," I said.

"Of course. It is a parent organization of ours, so I can actually set up a new account for you, or we can roll it into an existing account," Daniel explained.

"A new account, please."

"Joint or personal?"

I looked at Emil and nodded at him to answer for us.

"Joint."

Daniel proceeded to take our personal information and within 10 minutes, the new account was created. He printed documents for each of us to sign, Janina with the signature of *K. Chereshenko*, Emil and I with our own names, to authorize the transfer of funds.

"Now the last step before we transfer the funds would be the painful part," Daniel snickered as we signed the papers one at a time. "If you know what I mean."

"Yes, of course," Janina said. "Was it just a finger prick, or saliva sample? I am forgetting now."

"Just a prick of the finger would be all I need. I'll send it to our lab technician, he'll do a quick match of the DNA to your account, and then we'll start the transfer of funds."

Daniel brought a small medical kit to the table, rubbed Janina's middle finger with an alcohol wipe, and pricked it. He dabbed the dot of blood against a small plastic receptacle, sealed it, and left the room.

As soon as he was out of sight, Golecki stood up, sighing nervously and walking to the panoramic window of the board room with his hands on his hips. Something on the street level caught his eye.

"We're going to need to move a little quicker," he said after a moment as he looked down from the window. Emil and I got up briskly to see what Golecki was talking about. Five stories below our board room, a grim Kalinka was getting out of a limousine and being escorted into the building by the three bodyguards we had seen the night before.

"Shit," I whispered. "We have to go."

We left the board room and bolted down the same hallway we had seen Daniel turn into. When we arrived at the elevator bank, we followed the signs that said *Laboratory* and opted to take the stairs instead of the lift to descend into the basement. Emil and Golecki sprinted ahead while I helped Janina down the stairs. She grimaced at almost every step, but knew she needed to keep up the pace.

We arrived at the lab and burst into the dark room, where Daniel was leaning against a counter next to a younger man dressed in a white lab coat, huddled over a laptop, a palette of dyes, and the plastic receptacle that contained Janina's blood sample.

"Darling!" Janina exclaimed walking towards Daniel and the lab technician. "Joanna just reminded me that our flight out is at fourteen-hundred hours, not nineteen-hundred. I completely forgot. See what my poor little head is doing to me?"

"But, Kalinka, the match hasn't been processed yet. I will have to ask that you stay until we process the sample," Daniel protested politely. "Just company protocol."

"Daniel, darling, couldn't you do me just this one favor? For this old, ailing woman who came all this way to see you?"

"It will only take a few minutes, I promise. As soon as we have confirmed it has matched, you can be on your way, I'll take care of the rest. Have a seat, relax. Can I offer you anything to drink? A water? A tea?"

Daniel gestured to the row of leather seats near the entrance of the lab, but we were too anxious to rest. Emil stood at the windows of the lab, which looked out into the hallway, and checked outside every few seconds for Kalinka and her entourage. After two more minutes, the technician finally spoke.

"Confirmed."

"Thank you, darling! Next time, I promise you a dinner. We'll be off now, take care!" Janina shouted behind her as we pulled her through the glass door and escaped the building using the nearest side entrance. The alarms began sounding as we stepped into the bank's alleyway behind the building.

"Split up. I'm taking Golecki and Janina back to Warsaw," Emil said, grabbing my wrist. He pulled me in for an unexpected, deep kiss, and then let me go, fleeing to the right. I checked behind me to make sure they kept moving and within seconds, they were out of sight.

As I turned to run to the left side of the alleyway, I saw three large figures round the back corner of the building and start in my direction. I spun around and ran the opposite way. They drew their guns and started yelling.

"Stop! Stop, or we'll shoot!"

I slowed to a walk, raising my hands in the air. If they had wanted me dead, they would have shot by now and left me in a dumpster behind the building.

One of the bodyguards apprehended me, leading me towards the main street in front of Zurich Swiss One and into the limousine. I smelled Kalinka's Dior perfume escape from the car before I even settled into my seat, and then found myself sitting across from her. Two bodyguards entered the back seat with us and flanked her on each side. The third bodyguard got into the driver's seat and sped away.

"You may have gotten on the wrong flight," Kalinka said. She was filing her nails and hadn't looked up at me once since I had entered the car.

"I was just making a pit stop on my layover."

"You're only in Zurich for one thing, and that's the money. I'm sure you figured out before we arrested you that Swiss banks secure their cash in an impenetrable way. Whatever you thought my password was, or whatever bank account number you thought you stole after being in the tunnel for all of 10 minutes, didn't work for you. So it's a shame you'll be dying for nothing."

"You're right, there was no password. Any code we provided to the banker didn't work," I conceded, stalling to allow Emil, Golecki, and Janina more time to get to the airport and to give Daniel time to move the funds. The longer I could let 570 million euros flow to the newly created joint account, the better.

"You are much stupider than I thought. I shouldn't have expected an average mathematician, much less a Polish-American, to somehow swindle me of my fortune. It's just too bad I have to eliminate you now. I gave you a chance to get out alive…"

"Oh, you must have misunderstood me," I said. The bodyguard had just turned onto the highway as we entered a traffic jam visible for at least the next kilometer.

"What did you say?" Kalinka asked, finally looking up from her nails, her piercing eyes on my face. She held the nail file rigidly in her right hand.

"I just said you must have misunderstood me. I didn't have the password, but that doesn't mean you still have your money."

Kalinka took a deep breath.

"What are you talking about?" She asked slowly, leaving any playfulness out of her tone.

I paused, reveling in the gratification of surprising Kalinka. She dropped the nail file into her lap, and I caught the slightest glimpse of her hands shaking. She took her phone out of her purse and scrolled through her contacts. She put the receiver to her ear as I heard the dialing tone.

"Kalinka, darling! Please tell me you are coming back to see me tonight so we can get that dinner you promised," Daniel's familiar voice echoed faintly from the phone against Kalinka's ear.

"Daniel, what did you just do with my money?" She was completely stoic.

"Oh, poor dear. I see what you mean about the Alzheimer's. You were just here, silly, with your daughter and her fiancé. We moved the cash to their joint account in advance of their upcoming wedding!"

"I see. And I signed the documents, and you took my blood sample?" Kalinka asked. Her voice was wavering.

"Yes, darling, the same drill as always. You can even ask Joanna. She should be right there with you. And come to think of it, it wasn't too bad of an idea, considering the news that came out of Poland yesterday morning. I know whenever I see those ominous headlines, you're the diva behind them! Smart of you to secure the money under a different account."

"And I came to you? You're sure it was me?"

"It was you, darling, Manolo Blahniks and all!"

Kalinka hung up the phone and dropped it into her lap against her nail file.

"Idiot," she whispered, putting her face gently in her hands. "I don't even wear Manolo Blahniks."

She took a deep, shaky breath. I knew this was a blow to her mental stability. After several seconds, she gathered herself and leaned forward towards me.

"I don't know what kind of imposter you set up to get those funds, or where you got a sample of my blood, but the bank will retract the transaction as soon as I go back to Zurich."

"Oh, I'm not sure… Not if they can trace back a terrorist attack and attempted governmental coup to you. I don't think the European Banking Authority would want to be tied up in that, since, like Daniel said, the plane crash has now made international news. He can only protect you so much. We both know he'd need EBA approval to circumvent security protocols and retract such a large transaction."

"They can't trace anything back to me." I knew she felt like her control was slipping through her fingers.

"The Polish government doesn't have much on you, but they have enough."

"I have more people working for me in Poland than you can imagine. If you only knew how decayed the government was. It's on its last legs. The plane crash was the final push, and now it'll all come tumbling down," Kalinka said confidently, leaning back in her seat, crossing her arms.

"And how do you think they'll react when all those people start calling you for their paycheck after the work they've done for you?"

Kalinka paused to consider that complication, and then, out of nowhere, a perplexing smile spread across her face.

"You silly, pretty thing…" She started. "Do you think I got to you without some help on the inside?"

I didn't understand her question.

"I thought I'd save this ace up my sleeve until a more appropriate time, but it doesn't really get more opportune than this."

"What are you talking about?" I asked.

"I told you I have people all over Poland. In the government, at the airport... even in your bed."

I bit my tongue and suppressed the urge to look away from her. She could have been bluffing, but if she wasn't, I didn't want to give her the satisfaction of upsetting me.

"Why do you think you weren't able to find someone at the SKW that could help you intervene this week? The only other person alive who knew about the tunnel was the man who came to Poland with you. If he knew the scientist, he could have known anyone at the agency. And how do you think we knew to wait for you in the tunnel yesterday? Did you actually think we were guarding our premises, guarding the modular reactor? You couldn't dream of disarming what we have, and you wouldn't think of destroying the tunnel."

I reconstructed the events of the past week in my head again and weighed the probability that Kalinka was telling the truth. I took my time thinking through Emil's behavior with me and considered perhaps the most unexpected development of the week – that he was suddenly enamored by me.

There were also conflicting indications that he might not, in fact, be working for Kalinka. He led us to Golecki after the failed attempt of luring Skiba in to intervene with Kalinka. He agreed with me when I suspected Marek was working on the inside with Kalinka. He didn't impede our integration of Janina into the Zurich plan. He helped us get to Zurich Swiss One and transfer all of Kalinka's assets out of her account.

But he moved them into a joint account. And then, he left me.

If he was working with Kalinka, it would go against every value that was ingrained in him throughout his upbringing, throughout his childhood with me.

I told myself to not be naïve. It could all have been a decoy. He could have been maintaining appearances towards me to keep me in Europe near Kalinka.

I stayed quiet as my mind vacillated between scenarios of Emil's involvement with Kalinka while we continued through construction in the stop-and-go traffic. I had just one question of honor that remained in my head and wanted to desperately answer for myself: if I were Dziadek, would I trust Emil anymore?

21

"I haven't left Europe and you haven't killed me yet," I finally spoke after over an hour of silence as we drove onto the tarmac of the airport.

"That's very true," responded Kalinka.

Her private jet was waiting in the executive terminal for us, ready to bring us back to Warsaw from Zurich. The pilot greeted us at the bottom of its carpeted stairs as we ascended into the plane. I was seated across from Kalinka, facing her in a leather chair adjacent to the line of windows.

She was immediately served a glass of tomato juice and a croissant that seemed to be so fresh it could have been baked by a French boulanger in a tiny kitchen somewhere in the back of the jet.

"Coffee? Juice? Champagne?" Kalinka offered as she gestured through the air between me and the stewardess. She took a long sip of her juice, then exhaled with satisfaction as she set her drink down on a tray table near the window. I declined, but I pulled out my water bottle I had been carrying around Zurich with me since we arrived at its airport a few hours ago. I wasn't about to accept a refreshment from her without knowing whether it had been poisoned already by the stewardess.

"Why are you bringing me back to Warsaw?" I asked. She knew she had lost her money, or perhaps she knew that Emil had transferred it to a joint account, and she could still access it if he was her pawn. Either way, she didn't have a need for me anymore. Her bodyguards could have had me killed in the Zurich Swiss One back alley and she could have been on her way, returning to the coup she was staging inside the Polish government.

"You've learned now that I know how to use people, darling. Skiba, Marek, Magda, Emil... and now, you."

"And you've learned by now that I would never do anything for you."

"Well, we'll see about that. Don't you at least want to hear your options?" Her sinister smile crept back onto her face as she brought a shred of her croissant to her lips, careful not to brush its crispy shell against her perfectly painted lips.

The pilot closed the door to the jet. The bodyguards made themselves comfortable in the three seats behind me, pulling out a deck of cards and opening a bottle of beer each. Soon we were on the runway and, moments later, climbing into the air through the clouds.

"As you may recall, among the very noble things your grandfather did for his country, one of the greatest historical questions he prompted with his memoir was the suggestion that he knew the whereabouts of three hidden nuclear warheads around Russia, discovered by the Poles during the war."

Goosebumps appeared down my arms. Of course I remembered. Kalinka was after his last unsolved mystery. Kacper hadn't come to my condo to look for papers on the tunnel. Whether or not he knew it, he had come to find maps of the warheads.

"And you want to know where they are."

"Yes! See, darling, I knew you weren't so dense. Brilliant conclusion, you took the words right out of my mouth," Kalinka said sarcastically, waving the stewardess over for a refill of her tomato juice. "You see, it's not just that I want to protect Russia from the imminent danger of their accidental explosions, it's that I'd love to leverage these artifacts of the war and repurpose them."

"For national defense and global chaos. You'd have no problem initiating the eventual collapse of mankind."

"Not necessarily. For scientific development, too. But perhaps, if there's ever an opportunity..." Kalinka gazed out the window, seeming to mull over my mention of a nuclear holocaust.

"And what makes you think I have the slightest idea where those are? The world's most renowned historians have gone through all of my grandfather's papers, and anything he left behind after his death has already been burned."

"You somehow deduced your way to the tunnel, didn't you?" Kalinka held up her cup for the incoming stewardess, her long plum-painted nails tapping against the glass of her drink.

"Even if I knew where he may have hidden the maps for the warheads, why would I turn those over to you? I'd rather die."

"Oh, I know. I wasn't going to bother to threaten you with death, we both know you have more honor than anyone on this plane right now. Even Evgeny over there used to be a Ukrainian patriot who swore he'd live and die for his country, and now he's like a well-fed dog at the feet of his master," Kalinka whispered as if she were spilling the latest high school gossip, then leaned out of her chair into the aisle and smiled at Evgeny, who laid down a card on the table and smiled back, ignorant to our conversation.

"What's your offer?" I asked.

"You find me the maps to the warheads, and I'll call off the coup."

So that was her entire scheme. She let me come to Europe, find my way to the tunnel, encounter her, and maybe even move forward with the plane crash and coup only to seek my help in finding the warheads that had been buried for almost 70 years. And she was morally blackmailing me into it. I was to choose between the preservation of the country my grandfather, and now I, fought for, or the empowerment of its nearest enemy.

"How can I trust you'll call off the coup if I find you the maps?"

"I'm powerful, darling, but there's only one of me. I can't run the revolution of a whole government and unearth a trinity of nuclear warheads all by myself. I'd rather protect Russia and lose this opportunity in Poland than gain a tiny country that I care so little about while foregoing my own homeland."

I was too conflicted in the moment to scoff at her use of the term homeland, knowing where she was born and withholding the truth about her actual nationality from her.

"Fine," I answered at last. I was going to finish the job I had come here to complete. Kalinka clapped excitedly and called for two flutes of champagne.

"Wonderful! Unfortunately, one of my flaws is that I am not a very patient person. So, you'll have three days after we return to Warsaw to find the maps, which I think is generous," she said as the stewardess approached with the tray of flutes and an unopened bottle of Moët & Chandon.

I didn't know what I had agreed to or how the next few days would unfold. All I knew was that I'd have to improvise along the way, and that I had to do it by myself.

22

We arrived at Chopin International two hours later. I promptly left the plane before anyone was able to stand from their seats and got into a black Mercedes that I was told would be arranged for me. I wasn't worried about Kalinka's entourage knowing where I was anymore. I was sure I'd be followed for the rest of my stay in Poland. I stepped into the car and stared out the window as Kalinka elegantly descended the stairs from her jet. She put her sunglasses on, waved at me with her ominous smile, and got into her own black Mercedes with her three bodyguards. Her car drove away, and our car followed.

I was taken by the chauffer to a hotel, where I found Emil waiting for me in the lobby. I suppressed an emotional eruption, knowing he had already been informed where I would be staying.

"What the hell do you think you're doing?" I asked, bewildered that he would think I would want to see him upon my return from Zurich.

"Don't listen to anything Kalinka told you," he said immediately.

"Why would I ever trust you now?" I didn't hold back my curtness with him.

"Joanna, let me explain. She came to me and wanted me to bait you towards her this entire week– "

"And you did a fine job of that. I'm in an even worse position now than I was when we arrived a week ago, no thanks to you. Now my hand has been forced and I'm helping the same person who blackmailed Dziadek and Magda their entire lives. Whether I chose to go home and let the coup run its course or stay here and get her the maps so Russia can regain control of their warheads, I'm helping Kalinka. Do you understand that? I don't have a choice."

"It's better than dying."

"No," I protested. "There are things worse than death."

The televisions in the hotel lobby were streaming live videos of the Chancellery building.

It was a chaotic scene of military personnel guarding the perimeter of the building while people, dressed from business suits to oil-stained overalls, were chanting and yelling in their faces. Half of the people were surely provoked by Kalinka, while the other half were joining in their idea of a revolution, swept up in the emotion of the riot. A few protestors were shown to break loose from the guards' security and began scaling the walls, breaking into the first story windows. I took a deep breath as I watched the video. I could stop this coup, but would the impact of that decision have even worse consequences on these people?

I pushed Emil away with my shoulder, and left the hotel, heading back towards the black Mercedes that brought me there. The chauffer scurried behind me to catch up, but I arrived at the car first. I took hold of the handle and let myself into the car, slamming the door shut behind me. I looked straight ahead, ignoring Emil's pained face as he approached the car.

"Warsaw Public Library," I said as the driver got into the car. We sped off onto the highway, separating Emil and I for the second, bitter time since we arrived in the same city a week before.

~ ~ ~

I stopped for lunch on the way to the library knowing I'd be there late, pondering the pages of my grandfather's war memoir until the building closed. I, like Emil, worked better on a full stomach.

I was directed to the section of the library titled *Polish History 1939-1945* and quickly made my way to section "S". It took less than a minute to find *On the Call to Vilnius* by Henryk Jerzy Sosna, where 10 copies were arranged in order of edition. I plucked a copy of the first edition from the shelf and brought it to one of the open tables that also housed a computer for public use. I set down my bag, took a pen and stack of blank papers from the nearby printer, and sat down. I felt like I was at the university library of the Sorbonne again, and welcomed the familiar academic surroundings of Europe. I smiled to myself, reminiscing my days as a student, then opened the book and began reacquainting myself with the words of my grandfather in the Letter from the Author on the first page: *"In the history of*

Polish armed forces during World War II, the Home Army's activity in Vilnius was just one episode; an important episode, but one that is increasingly forgotten…"

When the library closed that evening, I registered with my passport for checkout and took the book with me outside. I was perhaps the last person in the building, other than the library manager and the janitors, who quickly locked the doors behind me once I departed.

Instead of heading back to the hotel, I went to a nearby bar for dinner and a drink. I was halfway through the densely written military history and needed to refuel before continuing through the memoir.

Hours later, the bar was closing early. I realized it was a Sunday night, but I still hadn't finished the book. I paid my tab and went outside, finding an empty bench on the side of the road to read the last two chapters over what remained of my pack of cigarettes.

The mid-April night was cold, but the warmth of my parka and the three beers I had drunk made me numb to it. My grandfather had taught me when I was a young girl that whenever I felt the slightest bit of discomfort, I should think about how much people before me had suffered. He reminded me that women were starved in concentration camps, men froze to death in the forests of the Soviet Union, and children were separated from their parents, sometimes forever. Suffering was relative. When compared to something worse, my pain easily disappeared.

With the final words on the last page, I decisively shut the book. I was now very tired. As if on cue, the familiar black Mercedes pulled up for me on the street and the last sentence of the memoir echoed in my mind: *"When they departed, they left a tremendous testament of their battle for their city, for Ostro Brama, for the Pearl of the Crown of Poland, for the Florence of the North, for Poland's Vilnius… for which they worked, fought, suffered, and gave their lives."*

It was those people, the deceased that my grandfather wrote about, and now he who would have to speak to me from beyond the grave. I was fighting for this country as they had. I stepped into the car and prayed that the words of the dead, together with the will of the living, could free Poland once again.

23

I spent the next day in the business center of the hotel I slept at the night before. I had reserved an entire office to myself, complete with a computer, desk, whiteboard, and writing utensils of every color, but all the resources in the world couldn't help me determine where to start in my research that day.

I was alone, so brainstorming with another individual was not an option. A sentimental side of me considered calling Emil, but as soon as I recalled he had probably been corrupted by Kalinka, I forced the idea out of my head and stepped outside for a cigarette to immediately refocus.

As I smoked on the sidewalk, trying not to mind the chauffer whom Kalinka had commanded to keep track of my whereabouts in Warsaw, I thought through the memoir I had read the night before. I had refamiliarized myself with it, but it was only for historical context and to jog my memory of the significant events in Dziadek's wartime experience that might assist in thinking through where he would have hidden the maps of the warheads.

Kalinka wasn't wrong when she mentioned the suggestion that Dziadek knew where the warheads were buried. In the ninth chapter, midway through the book, he described "cement-encapsuled tombs for their bodies, whose impact, if detonated, would be incomprehensibly devastating." They were "scattered around the land of the enemy, like tiny seeds waiting to bloom into calamitous, annihilating weeds."

According to the memoir, there had been a small, covert team of Soviets who had transported three warheads from a central laboratory in Moscow and coordinated their concealment during the war. He noted that one of the great successes of the Polish underground forces was that a group of them were spying on this Soviet team. The Poles would follow them, note the burial ground for each warhead, and then assassinate them and confiscate their documents around the locations of the warheads. The mission was top secret on the Soviet side, so the Russians would be able to find the warheads. There was even the presumption that some of the warheads had been carefully removed and reburied by the Poles during the Cold War. My grandfather, in his memoir, alluded that those men reported to him.

The language around the warheads, however, was interpreted by many historians to be more literary rather than literal. With his early onset Alzheimer's in the 1980s, many even thought that Dziadek had imagined the entire concept and transcribed it from a hallucination. He didn't include any names of those individuals and the chapter on the warheads was a suspicious, but short one. The case on the warheads, for many skeptics who had read *On the Call to Vilnius*, was closed.

There was another group of his readers, however, who insisted that this mystery of the hidden warheads was not a conspiracy theory but historical fact. I remember my grandfather receiving stacks of letters from readers in both Poland and the United States, asking him to divulge the whereabouts of the weapons. "If you were a true patriot, you'd tell international authorities where they are," they would usually say. Whether by personal choice or due to his inability to remember details from the past, he would ignore the requests, shred the letters, and throw them in the garbage.

I didn't necessarily fall into either category. Seeing my grandfather in all stages of his Alzheimer's, I wouldn't have been surprised if it was a figment of his imagination, but I also knew that if he was able to hide the truth about the tunnel for so long, he could have been hiding the warheads.

Kalinka, it turned out, fell into the category of the people who believed the warheads did still exist, and she wasn't going to risk letting the one person who might be able to infer their locations get away from her. She had nothing to lose by forcing me to help her, and everything to gain.

I started that morning in the hotel's business center using a different approach than the day before. I had a latte in my hand and had not yet opened the book. The sun from daybreak fell into the window-rich office. I stared through the window outside at the flow of Varsovians on their way to work, thinking through the possibilities of how Dziadek may have encrypted something about the warheads and whether there was even anything for me to decode.

I thought through the two remaining articles that remained from him – the letter I had read at his funeral and his memoir. I had kept his letter near me this entire trip and pulled it out of the breast pocket of my blazer, flattening it out on the desk and rereading it, perhaps for the hundredth time that week. Without learning any new hints, I leaned back in my chair and sipped on the latte again, reverting to my gaze through the window.

There was one more piece of writing that referred Dziadek, but it wasn't written by him. It was written by me. I pulled out my phone and scrolled to the Notes app, opening the draft of the eulogy I had given at his funeral, prompting me to think about his life. I read my opening line out loud in the office.

"Today we bid farewell to Colonel Henryk Jerzy Sosna. He was a family man, a friend, an expert card player when he had his fill of vodka, an immigrant with a gritty work ethic, and a national hero…"

Cards.

It was a strong passion my grandfather had cultivated after moving to America, but it was something others wouldn't have known if they hadn't met him personally. I thought through the games he frequently played against Wujek, his other Polish friends living in Chicago, and even against me. It seemed to be the single activity he clung to in his old age. Even his Alzheimer's couldn't vacate the memory of playing cards from him.

There was one game he defaulted to in particular. It was originally an Italian game, called Scopa. He had learned it from other soldiers who had spent time in Italy fighting for General Anders's army during the Battle of Monte Cassino and then returned to Poland at the end of the war, joining his unit in Wachlarz. He loved the game so much that he continued to play it against his Italian neighbor in Chicago, who had immigrated from Sicily around the same time my grandparents came to the United States. Dziadek would go to Sergio's house or Sergio would come to his house almost every weekend for a few rounds of Scopa before their wives would remove the vodka and wine from the table and shoo their husbands to bed.

I set my latte down and shuffled around the drawers of the desk in the office, sorting through notepads, reams of printer paper, and pens, until I got lucky and found that the bottom drawer of the desk was reserved for games. I took the deck of cards sitting on the top of the chess board, shut the drawer, and started dealing on the desk to initiate a game of Scopa between me and myself.

In Italy, one could find a unique deck of cards that was made for Scopa with the traditional suits drawn on each card. I bought a few decks in Venice when I visited during my time at the Sorbonne and brought them back to Dziadek for Easter break that year as a souvenir. He was thrilled, and he even gifted one of the decks to Sergio, who hadn't seen the Italian-made cards since he left the country after the war.

But Scopa could also be played using a traditional deck of cards, if the numbers eight through ten of each suit were removed, leaving 40 cards in the deck, which was also called a Milanese deck. Each round of Scopa was played, and points were tallied, until the first player reached twenty-one points. Points were earned for every "sweep." A sweep occurred when the cards on the table were cleared by either matching them with the cards in a player's hand or removing the cards whose sum totals a card in the player's hand. There were additional points earned for special rules, such as for the player who captured the most cards or the player who captured the most sevens.

Seven was the divine number in the game of Scopa. Not only were extra points awarded to the player who captured the majority of the four possible sevens contained in the Milanese deck, but they were also awarded to the player who captured the *sette bello*, or the seven of diamonds.

I stood up and walked to the whiteboard in the office and started transcribing the scoring table of Scopa onto its surface so I could create a visual representation of the rules.

1 point for the greatest number of captured cards

1 point for the greatest number of diamond cards

1 point for the seven of diamonds

1 point for the *primiera* – the player who obtains the highest sum of the highest scoring cards, one from each suit

> Determination of the *primiera*:
> Sevens - 21
> Sixes - 18
> Aces - 16
> Fives - 15
> Fours - 14
> Threes - 13

Twos - 12

Face cards – 10

Once I had the scoring written out, I was able to clearly see the numbers and start rearranging them in my head, based on patterns that seemed to be organized into a logical order or direction. Just like I had considered phone numbers, bank accounts, and coordinates with the page numbers where we found the word Magda in the war memoir, I started doing the same with the scoring table for Scopa.

Regardless of the number of sweeps or the number of cards captured by a player during each game, which could vary depending on the game, it was certain that any player who captured all four sevens would automatically score a point for the *primiera* and a point for the seven of diamonds. Even if that player were disadvantaged in every other factor of the game, the extra points could still be earned and usually put the player on top. Four sevens, each scored at twenty-one points in the *primiera* tally, would give the player half of the four possible extra points.

Four. Seven. Twenty-one.

I stepped away from the whiteboard and stared at the numbers I had jotted. They didn't mean anything yet but surmising how my grandfather might code the place where he hid the maps to the locations of the warheads would take time. I picked up my latte and collapsed onto the chair.

Four. Seven. Twenty-one.

The familiar sequence of numbers made me pause. These were the highest scoring *primiera* numbers in my grandfather's favorite game, and I was the only living person to know that. But there was something in those numbers that reminded me of another whisper from the past. I stood up again and went to the whiteboard, writing out the numbers 4-7-21.

The date April 7th, 1921 would have been insignificant to me, if I were thinking like any other American. I suddenly realized, however, that the format of the date was wrong. I had to think like a European, who would consider the first digit the date of the month, not the month of the year.

July 4th, 1921.

That whisper from the past was not my grandfather's eulogy, but my grandmother's. My mind flashed back to her funeral at Trójcowo and how my eulogy started, very blandly, with her birthdate, as if I were reading from a Wikipedia page. *"Magda was born on July 4th, 1921 in the small village town of..."*

It dawned on me that my grandfather clung to the game of Scopa, especially during the war, because he was separated from his wife. The highest scoring numbers, a combination of the four sevens, which each earned twenty-one points, reminded him of her while they were apart, suffering in different parts of the country.

Another detail of my grandparents' funerals made me pause. I returned to the desk where the flattened latter from my grandfather lay, reading the sentence about Magda again: *"Magda, you were the key to my life. With you, I could unlock all things, escape from all things, see all things, and love all things."*

Janina's mother wasn't the only key that would help us unlock the mysteries that lie in the tunnel. My grandmother was, too. He loved both of them until the end of his life, even if he couldn't speak of the Magda he left behind in Poland to Magda, his wife.

My eyes scanned the rest of the letter from Dziadek and stopped at one of the last sentences: *With my war memoir, I want to be a bridge between what lives and what has passed.*

Not only was his war memoir a bridge, but so were his wife, his lover, his passions, and his life.

I realized I didn't need him alive to be able to discover everything I needed to know about his secrets, which I thought had died with him. He left everything I needed to know in his book and in the way he lived his life, which I grew up observing closely and loving.

I also knew that if there truly were maps that were buried, the only place they could be was the same place for which he fought and wrote his memoir. They weren't in Poland, and they weren't in Russia. They could only be in Lithuania.

24

I peeked through the window of the business center office to make sure the black Mercedes with the chauffer-potentially-bodyguard was still parked around the corner of the hotel, as it had been the night before when it had dropped me off. After I confirmed the car's position, I erased the whiteboard and went to the hotel's receptionist to ask if they could arrange a rental car for me to use for the rest of the week.

Within half an hour, I had changed into athletic clothing, something I would not usually wear in public while in Poland, but for the sake of escaping the hotel without being noticed, I sacrificed conceit for my appearance. I paid the deposit for the car, intentionally using my newly issued debit card from Credit Suisse. The receptionist handed me the keys, and, when the chauffer in the black Mercedes was looking down at his phone, I pranced discretely from the lobby of the hotel into the parked Toyota. Within minutes I was on the highway, heading north again to the tripoint.

Knowing there could be another rendezvous with Kalinka in the tunnel between now and my deadline tomorrow, I decided to finally call the one person who might still be able to help me.

"You made it back to Poland?" Golecki asked abruptly as he answered my call.

"I even got here on a private jet."

"What are you still doing in Europe? The cash is transferred, you're rich now. You can do whatever you want."

"Except for the fact that I either need to stop a *coup d'état* or prevent a volatile nuclear state from acquiring three additional warheads."

I spent the next 20 minutes recounting the events that he had missed the day before after he, Emil, and Janina managed to escape from Zurich without being noticed by Kalinka. He remained silent until I had finished explaining every relevant detail, and then I made my request.

"Golecki, I need you to come to the tripoint. We need to disarm the reactor, and you're the only person I know who can do it."

"I knew this request was going to come from you," Golecki sighed. "When do you need me there?"

We arranged for him to leave work as soon as possible and to bring Janina with him. She wouldn't be able to provide much tactical help on either Golecki's side of disarmament or my side of finding the hidden maps of the warheads, but I feared that she might be in danger having been to Zurich, posing as Kalinka. If there was someone in the world identical in appearance and DNA to Kalinka, she no doubt would have wanted that person destroyed.

"And Golecki?"

"I'm listening." I had his attention for one more instruction.

"Whatever you do, don't involve Emil."

~ ~ ~

It was midday by the time I approached the recognizable intersection on expressway DW651. I drove past Café Gadam with my sunglasses on and noted several cars outside the normally vacant restaurant. Kalinka was boosting security around the Polish entrance to the tunnel. That was Golecki's problem, which I hoped he would figure out how to circumvent, either by finding another trustworthy resource within his division at the SKW or by going in disguise. The greater concern was that Kalinka's bodyguards knew what I looked like and there was no possibility of me entering Café Gadam and coming out alive. I'd have to try an alternative route, and it would have to be one I hadn't accessed before.

I continued driving, watching the intersection disappear in my rearview mirror. The entrance to the tunnel on the Lithuanian side was, at most two kilometers away. I fished out my passport from the glove compartment and drove along DW651 to the next border checkpoint, then crossed from Poland into Lithuania for the first time in my life. It was as close as I had ever been to the very city my grandfather fought for. Every kilometer I drove was taking me closer to Vilnius and closer to the side of the tunnel where I hoped the maps of the warheads were truly hidden.

25

I passed the security checkpoint at the Polish-Lithuanian border and I called Golecki immediately. I anticipated he had already arrived at Café Gadam, since he noted he would leave Warsaw promptly after my first call.

"How does Janina look? Hopefully more disheveled and back to her normal self. We don't want anyone thinking she is Kalinka's doppelganger."

"She's got her glasses on and no makeup. Her outfit is much... looser than how we dressed her in Zurich. Frankly, she looks like a peasant," said Golecki, speaking on the phone in the same car as Janina herself. I ignored his callousness.

"When you get to Café Gadam, enter separately. Let her go in first and get settled. She doesn't need to go into the tunnel, she just needs to stay close to us so we can get her out in case anyone suspects anything. There are at least five cars parked outside of the restaurant," I explained. "Do you have backup?"

"Yes."

"And just how did you find someone at the SKW that you trusted enough with this?"

"Well…" His pause made me uneasy. "He's not exactly part of the SKW."

I moved my phone away from my ear, gripping it tightly to release my frustration with his inference. I rubbed my temples with my other hand, then quickly replaced it onto the steering wheel.

"Please don't tell me you called Emil."

"Joanna, listen to me. Whether or not he's working for Kalinka, he is our only hope to get past the bodyguards and into the tunnel. He can convince them that I'm working on Kalinka's side, too, and I'm a developer coming in to check on some issues with the computer that controls the reactor."

"Goddamn it, Golecki, I told you to leave him out of this part."

"He's in a car behind me, so he's not here, but I'm going to tell you my honest opinion of him, Joanna. I don't think he's working for Kalinka."

"For all I know, you could be working for her, too."

"Do you have a choice right now but to trust both of us?"

I knew the answer was no. It seemed that everywhere I turned, I was being cornered into decisions. I didn't have any room to budge, but the end goal was to stop the cataclysm of events that had occurred since the plane crash. A coup was developing in Warsaw, and if I didn't turn over the maps of the warheads to Kalinka, there would be no chance I could prevent her organization from serving as the main vein for the Russian takeover of the entire Polish government.

Furthermore, we had already taken her assets in Zurich, but if we could disarm the nuclear reactor and prevent her from generating her main source of income, she and her organization would be completely deprived of power. If everything went perfectly, we could annihilate the entire threat and end the coup that very same day.

"Get into the tunnel," I started saying slowly through clenched teeth. "And override their system. Remove the rods and get the hell out of there as fast as you can." I hung up and dropped my phone into the empty passenger seat, rubbing my temples again with my free hand.

I had been in Lithuania for all of three minutes and realized that I had no idea where the shaft into the tunnel might be on this side of the border. Janina and Magda indicated that the distance from the vertex to either end of the tunnel was one or two kilometers. I pulled over on the side of the road and took a map from the side pocket of the driver's door, opening to the page with a zoomed-in aerial view of the tripoint area. I pulled the bottom button of my parka loose and unraveled the thread that had held it to my coat. Holding the thread taut, I placed it against the map's scale and wrapped one end of it around a pen until the distance between the other end of the thread and the point of the pen was equal to the scale's measurement of one kilometer.

I pinned the loose end of the makeshift geometric compass with my finger to the exact place on the map where Café Gadam was located, along DW651. I traced the circumference of a circle with the pen, using my finger as its center and the thread as its radius. I then repeated the same exercise with the same center, but with a two-kilometer radius. Once I removed the thread from the map, I retraced the annulus of the concentric circles, and cut off that area at Lithuania's borders. I was left with a small sector of the annulus on the northernmost part of the map that narrowed down the geographic area where the entrance to the tunnel in Lithuania might have been.

I didn't have a ruler or an accurate compass, but I estimated that if the Lithuanian border made about a 90-degree angle with Café Gadam, then the part of the annulus that lay in Lithuania was about 2.356 square kilometers. On the map, the angle even seemed a few degrees more acute than a right angle, so the area could have been less. The area was relatively small, but I was alone and only had until the end of the next day to find the maps. If I considered Kalinka's impatience, I had maybe even less time, and if the past week had proved anything, it was that she could show up unexpectedly anywhere she liked.

I got back on the road and started driving further north until I was certain I was fully inside the quarter of the annulus I had traced on my map. The map wasn't detailed, but there was very little to showcase in this part of the country anyway. I looked around and was surrounded by a forest of towering white birch trees. I stayed on the road for another minute, and then realized that 60 seconds of driving at my speed would have taken me outside of the circumference of the outermost circle I had drawn on my map.

I sighed, not having seen any landmarks, buildings, signs, or people, then turned my car around and headed back south into the quarter of the annulus I knew I needed to be investigating. I drove a kilometer on the same road and didn't notice anything different than my original one-minute drive north. Just trees in a forest.

I repeated this circular drive up and down the main road five times, turning back and forth over the one kilometer stretch and dreading the idea of potentially leaving my car and venturing into the damp, grey woods on foot. Every time I drove back down the road, my focus was more and more honed on the details of the woods – the way the sun fell through the trees, the cracks in the asphalt, the roadkill on either side of the road, the locations of the puddles from the recent rainfall.

I eventually rolled down my window to smoke one last cigarette before getting out of the car to scavenge on foot. As soon as the fresh, humid air rushed into the car, I finally noticed something different along a short section of the road. The scent that drifted into the car with the gentle breeze wasn't just from the residual warm rain. I realized I sensed the unmistakable, overwhelming aroma of pine.

I stopped the car in the middle of the road and pulled the key out of the ignition. Stepping out of the car, I turned towards the forest. Amid the tall birches, I saw a family of deep green pine trees. Over a dozen regal, full bodies stood not 20 meters from the side of the main road. I slammed the car door shut and marched between the birches towards the pines, and on my walk, I realized why I knew the entrance to the tunnel had to be there.

Sosna was the pseudonym that my grandfather carried during the war and eventually took on as his legal surname, which was passed down to me, in the United States.

Sosna was the Polish word for pine.

I approached the pine trees and noticed they were all the same height. I ran my hands along their prickly needles and peered through their branches to observe their trunk. I recalled from the summer self-defense camps I attended in high school that during survival week when we lived in the woods as scouts, we were instructed how to estimate the age of a tree. The same question was in the completion exam we had to pass at the end of the camp to earn a certificate.

The age of a pine tree is about two times its diameter in centimeters.

I guessed that the diameters of these pines were no less than 30 centimeters. They would have been just over 60 years old.

They were exactly the age I expected. Dziadek and his platoon planted these trees to mark the tunnel's Lithuanian shaft.

26

I pushed the branches of the pine trees aside and walked through their clearing until my footing changed and I was stepping on ground that was more solid than the rain-soaked soil of the forest. I crouched to the ground and started clawing at the thin layer of grass until, just a finger's depth from the surface, I was pulling back a layer of sod that covered a metal latch door like the one in Café Gadam. It didn't have a lock on it, which I guessed was probably for ease of access for Kalinka's mules. The remoteness of the location didn't necessitate a lock, either. Since I had driven into southern Lithuania, I hadn't seen a single other car.

I dug my fingers into the gap where the latch door met the soil and rose to my feet, lifting the door until it fell to the opposite side of the hole in the ground. I peered into the hole, lit by the sunlight coming through the branches of the pine trees, and saw the exact same shaft as the one beneath the floorboards of Café Gadam.

I descended the creaky wooden ladder, which most likely hadn't been replaced since my grandfather's platoon set it there, until I reached the floor of the tunnel. I used the screen of my phone to illuminate my path, but before I started walking into the darkness, something to my right caught my eye. I turned my phone to a small section of the dirt wall next to the ladder and, in a tiny space before the shotcrete started to cover the earth, I noticed the deep engraving of a cross. Below the cross, the number *1946* was also rudimentarily engraved, like a modern hieroglyph.

I ran my fingers over the cross and remembered that in this Lithuanian side of the tunnel, the Soviets carried out the massacre of Dziadek's platoon, leaving only him and Magda as survivors. Their mutual survival, their desperate attempt to escape from the tunnel alive, made even more sense now. Whether or not Dziadek knew it, Magda was pregnant. They wanted to survive together. Magda would be reminded of the slaughter every time she passed through this end of the tunnel as she transported narcotics or weapons or people to and from Poland. She buried her colleagues, her friends, with Dziadek in this forest and memorialized their deaths with this subtle symbol. She memorialized them with this cross. It may have been an homage to them, or it may have just been penance for her.

Did they forgive themselves for living while the others had died? I wondered if Magda despised her choice, knowing that one of her daughters would eventually be taken by the Soviets and rise as their leader. I wondered if I would have made a more noble decision than them. I wondered, if I was in her position, would the responsibility to my lover and my children have outweighed my responsibility to Poland, which I had taken an oath to protect? In the end, which was more important? Honor to country, or honor to family?

I turned back towards the tunnel, the gravity of the platoon's massacre still on my mind, and began walking south. I shook the haunting thought, reminding myself that I still needed to find the maps.

Four. Seven. Twenty-one.

If the maps were on this side of the tunnel and the numerical code meant anything, I could only guess they were distances, measured in the metric system. There were various combinations that I could attempt. The maps could be buried twenty-one meters into the tunnel, seven centimeters from either wall, and four centimeters beneath the surface of the dirt. The variations, especially if I considered that it could be measured from either wall, the floor, or the ceiling and that it could be measured in meters or centimeters, would have led me to dig for days. I had neither the equipment nor the time to spare for such a venture.

After exhausting the iterations of the 4-7-21 code in my head, I turned around and started walking back towards the shaft I had originally entered. Suddenly, I heard a whirring noise coming from behind me. I turned around to see what was approaching and, seeing nothing through the darkness, I started running. Before I got to the ladder, the bright beams of headlights fell onto my back and the surrounding shotcrete walls of the tunnel. I spun around just as the whirring stopped, seeing a small electric cart parked in front of me. In the cart were Kalinka's three bodyguards and, with them, Janina and Emil.

Emil and I locked eyes over the headlights. I wanted to express too many feelings towards him – confusion, affection, pain, desperation – but his stare only declared one thing to me: atonement.

Before that moment, I hadn't known how to see an apology in just a face. An apology was something uttered, something discussed at length. It was something given by one person and received by another. In Emil's eyes, though, I saw his remorse, not for having done anything wrong, but for having lost my trust. He knew honor was the single most important value to me. He looked as if he had lost it and wanted nothing more than to gain it back.

Golecki was gone, meaning he was either captured separately, he had been killed, or he had gotten away. I wouldn't have blamed him for leaving the scene. His nerves wouldn't have held up in the laboratory and there was a chance that, if things went wrong, he'd be notoriously considered a national criminal for setting off a nuclear explosion for decades after his death.

The bodyguard behind the steering wheel pulled out a phone and began speaking in Russian. I was only able to pick up a few words from the familiar Slavic language, but I knew he was reporting his arrest of us three to Kalinka. Within minutes, another cart came whirring through the dark tunnel and parked behind the first one. Kalinka stepped out of the vehicle, tugged at the long sleeves of her form-fitting black dress, and walked towards me without even looking into the other cart.

"Back so soon?" She asked me, stopping in front of the cart, the headlights beaming past her. "I assume this means you've found the maps."

"I still have all day tomorrow."

"Yes, but since you're here today, we can finish this now. There are only so many places the maps can be hidden. Where are they?" Kalinka asked. She was more grim than usual. Her patience was wearing thin.

"I need more time."

"Ah. Well, then, I'll give you a few more minutes. In the meantime, let's have a look at our friends we picked up at Café Gadam, hm?" Kalinka crossed her arms, turned around smugly, and walked to the other cart. When she saw Janina, her arms dropped to her side.

"I found her," Emil said, referring to Janina. "She escaped back to Poland after Zurich, but I located her address and brought her to you."

"You…" Kalinka started speaking as she examined her lookalike in the cart. I caught a hint of vulnerability in her voice. She cleared her throat, noticing it, too, then went on. "You posed as me at the offices of Zurich Swiss One. And now you've come here to die."

"Listen to me– " Janina began to speak from the cart.

"I cannot have another person in this world running around looking like me. There can only be one of me," Kalinka said. "Yury!"

The bodyguard behind the steering wheel got out of the cart and pulled a pistol from his holster.

"I'm not just another person," Janina said, standing up slowly. She held her injured torso as she stepped over the lap of the other bodyguard and exited onto the dirt floor, standing in front of Kalinka and staring into her eyes resolutely. "I am your sister."

Kalinka stepped back and looked Janina up and down.

"I don't have a sister."

"And not just a sister. An identical twin," Janina added. Kalinka stared at her counterpart as if she were disgusted with what she saw in the mirror.

"You used my DNA, my blood, to transfer the funds in Zurich."

"And you used our mother to commit crimes against humanity."

Janina's rebuttal sent Kalinka back another step. She blinked rapidly, as if to see her sister better. Kalinka tore her gaze from Janina and started looking between me, Emil, and her bodyguards.

"Kill them. All three of them. Right here," Kalinka demanded coldly.

The remaining two bodyguards got out of the cart and pulled out their pistols.

"She sacrificed her entire life. She sacrificed the safety of her country and any duty she vowed to it in order to keep me and you alive!" Janina yelled as the guards herded Janina and Emil towards the shaft of the tunnel where I stood. "She loved you even if you had been taken from her, Kalinka. She stayed in that tunnel to be able to see you, her daughter."

Janina's emotions started to spill out as a final attempt to save us and to convert her estranged sister. There was a moment of pause in Kalinka, a split second where she stared at the ground, unable to look directly into Janina's eyes, as if she had been embarrassed by how she had treated her mother and, perhaps, as if she felt some remorse.

Maybe this is it. Maybe we don't need to destroy everything Kalinka has created. Maybe she can dismantle it herself.

The moment passed as quickly as it came, though, and Kalinka raised her eyes to Janina again.

"Magda was my servant, not my mother. I have no mother, just as I have no sister."

The guards pushed us together to line us up at the shaft of the tunnel, the same place where, 64 years ago, their countrymen cornered my grandfather's platoon.

"Don't you want the maps?" Emil asked desperately.

"If the maps are in this tunnel, I will find them myself."

"And the coup?" I asked in the same panicked tone as Emil had used. Every hour I spent searching for the right answers to bring to Kalinka since I had returned from Zurich had now gone to waste, and the possibility of having her call off the takeover of the government was evaporating.

"You didn't hold up your end of the deal, darling," Kalinka responded. "Turn around."

"Give me one more chance. I know where they are," I was about to gamble our lives away, but if it bought me a few more minutes, there was still a chance I could stumble upon whatever my grandfather had buried. "If I don't find the maps, you can shoot us."

Emil turned to look at me, his eyes now screaming, *"What are you doing?"*

The silence from Kalinka implied her acceptance of my offer. I walked back to the cross I had found engraved in the wall, my only hope, and dug in the pockets of my parka for anything I could use to stab at the dirt. I was breathing so heavily, I was sure everyone in that tunnel could hear me. I took out my Zippo lighter and used its butt to start chipping away at the engraving.

Pieces of dried dirt began falling to my feet as the engraving of the cross and *1946* eroded with them. It took me two minutes to create a hollow that was three centimeters deep in the wall. Then, with one final jab, I heard the casing of the lighter hit a metal surface with a dull *clang*. I turned to look at Kalinka, whose interest I had piqued with the sound I had just made. Her eyes met mine, and she came to join me at the dirt wall.

I dropped the lighter into my pocket and started scratching at the remaining dirt, soon revealing a metal case. The dry dirt came loose around the case, which could then be easily pulled from the rectangular hollow in the wall. Before I could finish pulling it out, Kalinka's hands were already around it, shaking it anxiously and listening for its contents.

"I knew it existed," she whispered to herself. As she adored the case, turning it over in her hands, I looked back inside the hollow to ensure there was nothing else I had missed. Deep inside the hole I had dug, behind the place where the case had sat for over 60 years, I noticed a large, dusty red button with wires protruding from it. The wires led into the dirt, attached to something beyond the visible area I had dug out.

"What's the code?" She asked, shoving the metal case back towards me, interrupting my observation. She had discovered a hefty lock on the box. I looked back at the case and, instead of taking it from her to unlock it myself, I kept her busy by dictating the code to her.

"Four..." I said. Kalinka spun the dial of numbers on the lock diligently.

I squinted inside the hollow at the hidden button again. With the faintest light from the headlights behind me, I was barely able to make out the words written in white beneath it: *DETONOWAĆ*.

Detonate.

"I don't have all day, darling, do hurry up now," Kalinka said anxiously.

"Seven..."

My grandfather had set up the tunnel to destroy it. He knew that he was digging into enemy territory and, in case the Soviets did find the tunnel, he had wired the passage to explode.

I had no idea where Golecki was and whether the control rods had been removed from the reactor yet. Was I willing to sacrifice myself and purposely set off a second Chernobyl in my own home country to stop Kalinka? It was a choice between removing the organization that had terrorized Poland for almost 70 years and risking the devastating consequences of a nuclear disaster over the Baltic states. It was a choice between stopping the history of this country in its tracks and changing its future for another century.

"Twenty-one..."

I looked back at Emil and Janina as Kalinka occupied herself with spinning to the final number. My eyes darted between them and the ladder. Emil and Janina nodded in acknowledgement of the directions I was giving. My eyes then met Emil's again as I tried to interpret his thoughts before Kalinka and the bodyguards noticed I had found a detonator. Just then, he mouthed the words: *"Do it."*

I heard the lock click open. Kalinka opened the top of the case.

I wanted to wait next to her for her to unfold the papers and see, finally, the answer to the last mystery encrypted in my grandfather's memoir. I wanted to know who had been right. Did the warheads exist, or was the entire theory wrongly interpreted by the world? But I had to set my curiosity aside and perhaps leave this one last secret with the dead, unsolved.

I reached into the hollow, firmly pressed the red button, and ran to the ladder after Janina and Emil. The bodyguards lifted their guns to shoot at us, but then became distracted with the loud sounds of explosions echoing through the tunnel in the distant darkness, from the direction of Café Gadam. They started babbling among themselves, confused, in Russian. The sides of the tunnel shook with the reverberations of the explosions and fragments of the shotcrete began falling from the ceiling.

"Go!" I yelled up the ladder at Janina and Emil.

As they climbed and the line of explosions came closer to us through the tunnel, I turned to look at Kalinka once more. She was kneeling on the ground, frantically unfolding the papers. She looked small and forlorn on the ground, her bodyguards behind her panicking and already moving towards the ladder that I had begun ascending. I paused for one second on the ladder, debilitated by her pitiful determination to save the maps of the warheads, if nothing else. She would rather have stayed in that tunnel and martyred herself in the name of misery than escape alive and live in defeat.

Her power, she knew, had finally been stripped from her, but her pride consumed her still.

Realizing the bodyguards were close behind me, I sped up the ladder behind Janina and Emil. I didn't worry about them shooting at us anymore; they were now just trying to save themselves, pathetically abandoning their master.

Janina and Emil were waiting at the top of the ladder, their hands extended towards me, and pulled me up from the shaft onto the ground. Emil lifted the heavy metal latch door from the ground and slammed it shut over the hole, sealing away everyone and everything that remained in the tunnel.

The three of us sprinted to the parked Toyota and got inside. I sat in the driver's seat, turned the car on, and advanced north, away from the tunnel, as fast as I could. I felt the earth beneath the tires shaking, as the ripple effect of the explosions reached the inside of the vehicle. Even my foot shook against the gas pedal as my speed climbed to 200 kilometers per hour. Seconds later, in my rearview mirror, I watched the explosions finally reach the pine trees we had just left. The ground of the forest imploded, sending smoke and debris high above the treetops.

27

My arms tingled with adrenaline for so long after I witnessed the implosion that I finally had to pull the car over. An assembly of cars labelled *POLICIJA* whizzed past our parked Toyota in the direction of the collapsed tunnel as Emil, Janina, and I sat in silence, trying to catch our breath from the frenzy of escaping our near death.

After several minutes, I finally dared to speak.

"There was no cloud," I said, referring to the mushroom-shaped smoke that I expected to protrude into the air following a nuclear explosion.

"If there had been a cloud, you wouldn't have lived to see it," Emil responded, still panting from the dash we made towards the car minutes earlier.

"How did you do it?" I asked. I unbuckled my seatbelt and turned in my seat, facing Emil to my right and Janina in the back of the car.

"It was Emil's idea," Janina said. "We ignored the suggestion that you gave to Golecki over the phone. Sorry."

"But it worked. What did you do?"

"Janina was our red herring," Emil said. "I came into Café Gadam with her as if I had just arrested her. I took her into the back kitchen where I knew the bodyguards all sat during the day and told them I found Kalinka's twin after she had left Zurich. In the kitchen, we noticed the control board, wired for detonation. I knew when you looked at me in the tunnel after pulling the box out for Kalinka, you saw the same thing."

"They were shocked to see me, naturally, and wanted to turn me in to Kalinka immediately," Janina continued.

"And while they were panicked about this discovery, they abandoned the restaurant and Golecki snuck into the lab," I finished the story, putting the final pieces together.

My breathing remained heavy as I started considering that my reaction was from the emotions of the week and not just my running to the Toyota. My chest tightened.

"I need to walk," I said, abruptly leaving the car. I slammed the door shut behind me and began down the main road, shoving my hands deep into the pockets of my parka.

"Joanna!" Emil called behind me, getting out of the car and jogging to my side. "Joanna, stop."

"I don't know what to think of you. You kept all this from me for the past week, ever since Kalinka first got in touch with you. I thought that..." I stopped speaking before I said something that would expose what had been on my heart.

"You thought what?" Emil asked. He took my arm and pulled me to a halt in the middle of the road. I was now facing him, exasperated. I couldn't hold back what I said next.

"I thought we would tell each other everything, starting with this trip. The good and the bad. I've lost everyone, Emil," my voice started shaking. "I have no siblings, no parents, and now, no grandparents. I barely have any friends. I know I have my honor, though, and I thought that after this trip, at least I would have you."

Emil's eyes stayed on me intently. If he had something to truly apologize for, his eyes would have been cast away from embarrassment in that moment. He was a proud man, but not an arrogant one. He knew when he needed to be humbled, and it started to comfort me that he wasn't being humbled in that moment.

"You do have me, Joanna. You'll always have me, to the ends of the earth. And I hope that I still have you." Emil stepped closer to me and took my face in his hands.

Tears flooded my eyes. I wanted to think it was from exhaustion rather than passion, but I couldn't suppress my love for him any longer. He saw I was searching for answers and started explaining himself before I could ask him to say anything.

"Kalinka got in touch with me as soon as we were on our way to Poland. She must have gathered from Kacper that both of us interrogated him. Kalinka tried to blackmail me into eventually leading you to her this week. She told me that if you didn't comply with getting her the maps to the warheads, she would kill you. I said that I knew you better than anyone alive and that death didn't scare you, not when it came to duty, which is why she changed her deal and offered to call off the coup instead of threatening you with your life," Emil explained. His eyes met mine. "I didn't play you, Joanna; I played her."

"How did you know I was willing to die for this?" I asked, wiping tears from my eyes.

"I didn't. But I knew I needed to protect you."

"What about Janina and the DNA test? Did she know about that?"

"She thought I had gone to Zurich to follow you, not help you, which is why I had us get on separate planes. I had to keep up my act."

"Did Marek know Kalinka was working with you? What about Skiba? Wouldn't they have noticed you?"

"No one. Everything Kalinka knew, she kept to herself. She was her own lockbox, and things operated very efficiently under that approach for decades. She never thought she could be defeated. She thought she could handle everything by herself, until you came to Poland and dismantled her."

Emil drew me in and kissed me. When he pulled away, he wiped away my tears with his thumb.

"I stalled to keep you here because I knew you could destroy her. I didn't tell you anything because I knew if I told you, you'd either cut me out or stop fighting for the truth. Honor is too precious to you to keep someone like me, tainted by Kalinka's touch, near you. But I sold you short, Joanna, and I'm sorry. I knew you could finally free this country from 70 years of servitude to the organization. And look…" He nodded his head at the rising smoke behind me. "You did."

"I didn't want to trust you," I said, looking into his eyes. "I didn't want to think you could break down these walls."

"If you let me in, I promise to never leave."

"And how do I know I can trust you when you say that?" I asked, allowing the slightest smile.

"I've kept you alive this whole time, haven't I?" He asked, hugging me close to his chest. I could feel the warmth of him against my bare cheek, red from the chill of the spring that lingered in those woods. "If that promise can last three generations, I can keep this one, too."

28

We dropped off Janina at her home in Suwałki, but not before she could stock our car with bottles of homemade liquors and fresh bread she had baked the night before. She jotted down her address and phone number on a piece of paper but begged us not to call her unless we were dialing from Poland next time we visited. She didn't want to pay long-distance fees.

Janina poured us a ceremonious round of shots from the same bottle of vodka we had opened with her mother the week before and, with tears in her eyes, sent us on our way back to Warsaw. She didn't need to say the words to communicate her gratitude to us for helping bring down the era of bondage. Even without her mother with her, she could now breathe freely, knowing her family and her country were no longer tormented.

Emil drove the Toyota back towards Warsaw, seeming to never let go of my hand, which he held in his lap. Before we could speak in our newfound privacy after leaving Suwałki, my phone rang in my pocket. It was Golecki.

"What is it?" I asked. "Are you okay?"

"I'm fine. The rods are back at TR-003. I had a shit time driving them from Café Gadam in my car. I thought that every bump I hit in the road was going to cause them to crack, but I got them to the director of the nuclear power plant."

"Thank God," I responded. It was the last bit of relieving news I needed to hear to know that everything had gone smoothly on the opposite end of the shaft prior to the tunnel's explosion. We had all escaped safely.

"Joanna, there's someone who wants to see you when you come back to Warsaw," Golecki said hesitantly.

"Who is it?"

"I'm hoping you'll oblige his request," Golecki said. "It's the prime minister."

"Why does he want to see me?" I asked. A bubble of panic rose in my chest. "Does he think I committed some kind of crime?"

"No, not that at all," Golecki paused. "He wants to meet with you to see if you'll consider a position with the Council of Ministers. I looked up the list of victims from the plane crash on Saturday. The former Minister of National Defense was killed."

I was too tired to process the unspoken proposition yet. I wish I hadn't heard Golecki say that before I was able to properly rest. I rubbed my forehead, longing for sleep.

"I don't even– "

"At TR-003, as I was delivering the nuclear rods, the director asked me about the operation and how we had found the small modular reactor. I told him the whole story of you coming here last week, the international chase through Zurich, Kalinka's involvement, everything. TR-003 is a high security establishment that must be monitored by the government, and the director has a direct line to the prime minister. He called him on the spot and arranged a meeting between you and Donald Tusk."

I digested the news from Golecki and wondered if, by any chance, this was another setup. But even if Kalinka still had operatives within the government, not only was she dead, but she now didn't have any funds with which to pay them. Moreover, her sole means of generating those funds had just been destroyed. I realized that anyone who was working for her would eventually fizzle out, especially if she kept all her contacts confidential, as Emil said. Every pertinent piece of information about the organization had died with her. She was so proud, she thought she was immortal.

"Golecki, what's the news with the coup?"

"The riots at the parliamentary building have ceased. There was a rising leader in the Senat who was most vocal this past week about forgoing the democratic process of selecting an acting president and setting up a new form of government. It would have been run by Kalinka. The leader left the country already. Skiba's gone, Jaworski's gone. People aren't getting paid, Joanna, it's been days since we've transferred the funds from Kalinka's account. It's over."

"Then I'll meet with Tusk," I decided after confirming the chaos had ended. "Tomorrow, as early as possible."

29

Emil and I would have traditionally dined that evening and indulged in the highest forms of celebration, eating at the most ostentatious restaurants and drinking the most lavish cocktails. Instead, we returned to Warsaw, found the nearest hotel, and fell asleep immediately.

The next morning, once again, we were without a fresh set of clothes. The shirts and pants we wore the previous day were coated in soot from the Lithuanian woods. Golecki set up a meeting at 9:00 between us and the prime minister, but that was well before any stores opened to the public on a weekday. The only option for new clothes was the tourist shop in the lobby of the hotel where we slept. The manager of the hotel let us inside and we each picked out our kitschy selection of t-shirts and pants before paying him generously in cash and then making our way to the Chancellery in the city center on Ujazdowskie Alley.

Emil and I checked in at the Chancellery's reception and sat down in the wooden chairs across from the main desk.

"I look like a goddamn clown," I said, crossing my arms over my chest to hide the bright red and white shirt with what seemed to have every city in the country listed alphabetically in the shape of a heart. "I'm about to be asked if I want to join the Polish Council of Ministers and I look like I raided a souvenir shop. He's going to think this is my first time in the country."

"Did you know you also have the lyrics to the national anthem written across your back?" Emil asked, peeking behind me. I rolled my eyes.

"You don't look much better," I asserted, nodding at his black *I Love PL* shirt.

"I don't think the prime minister is going to dismiss the woman who just vanquished the greatest threat to this country's national security since the Cold War based on what she's wearing today," Emil whispered, leaning over to me. "Especially since you just blew up the tunnel less than 24 hours ago."

"Miss Sosna?" A woman appeared in the lobby holding a portfolio. "With me, please."

We were escorted into a conference room and, before we could seat ourselves, the glass door opened, and we were standing in front of Donald Tusk. He looked exactly as I imagined he would from my perceptions of him on the Polish news that I watched every morning from my condo. I never dreamed I would be meeting him in person, but the theme of the week was that reality exceeded all expectations.

"Miss Sosna and Mister Łowicki. What a great pleasure to meet you," Tusk shook our hands and gestured to the table for us to be seated. "My meetings generally run fifteen minutes long and I am shockingly on time for this one. Usually, I'd be five minutes late already, but here I am. And in the presence of such patriotically dressed individuals! You are like a postcard."

"The pleasure is ours, sir," I said, shaking his hand. "Please excuse the outfits. We were searching desperately for clothes this morning, I hope you understand."

"Of course, I understand. I apologize for the joke, it amused me."

"We will come in suits next time," I promised.

"Don't fluster yourselves. I'm going to be brief and get straight to the point. I won't give you any background because you can read about it in the news, but our Minister of National Defense was killed in the plane crash on Saturday. We need a new one and, as you know, our resources are limited. Now that Kalinka has been taken down, we just need the bad apples that remain in our government to rot into the ground. They'll go away by themselves if they're not being paid. But we are looking to fill the vacancy now with someone who is trusted, even if they serve as an interim minister. I pose this question to you, and you can take some time to think about it. Miss Sosna, I am offering you the position of Minister of National Defense."

Tusk spoke quickly and left no time for interruptions. Such was the life of a politician, quickly moving from one meeting to the next, attempting to maximize diplomatic arrangements in each one. Typically, I would have needed time to weigh my options and draft a calculated response, but since Golecki planted the idea in my head with his phone call yesterday, I had taken every waking moment to think about the opportunity.

"*Panie Premierze,*" I started, addressing him by his formal title. "I must respectfully decline your request. I would be happy to offer another trusted name for the position, as I know you are searching desperately to fill the position, but we will be returning back to Chicago this week."

I pulled a notepad and pen from the middle of the conference room table towards me and wrote down Golecki's phone number, then tore the sheet from its binding and handed it to Tusk. He looked at my note and nodded in acceptance of my resignation.

"Very well, I understand completely, Miss Sosna. I do have one gift for you, though, before you leave." Tusk turned to the glass door and motioned for his secretary to enter. She was holding a small velvet box. She set it on the table in front of him. I knew what it contained before she even opened the box for Tusk.

"Is that…"

"The Virtuti Militari medal," Tusk finished my sentence. "It hasn't been awarded since the Cold War. But then again, an enemy of the state has not been defeated like this since the Cold War. After communism fell, the Sejm passed a law, which prevented this award to be given within five years after the end of hostilities between

Poland and the aggressor, but special approval was sought this morning for you."

"My grandfather received one. He was buried with it at his funeral." I couldn't stop looking at the regality of the glistening medal. In the center of the cross, a golden circle donned a white eagle surrounded by laurel leaves. On top, a jeweled crown connected the dangling cross to the magnificent purple ribbon. The medal was identical to the one I had attached to Dziadek's uniform before his wake.

"Your grandfather, Miss Sosna, was a national hero," the prime minister said. "This week, you've become one, too."

Tusk rose from his seat and I stood to meet him.

"I, Donald Tusk, the fourteenth Prime Minister of Poland, award you, Joanna Sosna, with the War Order of Virtuti Militari for exemplifying virtue and finally freeing our nation." He pinned the ribbon of the medal to the left side of my chest as my eyes stung with tears.

I looked around the room where I stood with Emil and the prime minister. I wondered if my grandfather had received his medal in a similar way – without publicity, cameras, or spokespeople and at the eclipse of a national crisis. It was a modest ceremony, but one that seemed even more distinguished in its humility. A hero without the grandeur of recognition.

"I have one more order of business, *Panie Premierze*," I said after I cleared my throat. I took my hand off the medal, which I had mindlessly been touching since it was pinned to my ridiculous shirt. Tusk sat down in his chair, folding his hands.

"Yes, of course," he said with a smile. "Anything for the first recipient of the award in over 20 years."

"It's regarding the funds we withdrew from Kalinka's accounts."

"I'm listening."

"We don't feel it is right for us to keep the money, even if it is in our joint account under our legal names," I started, glancing at Emil.

"We'd like to transfer the balance of the cash and investments back to the Polish government, where it belongs," Emil added.

"I'm sorry, I was not aware that cash was involved. I don't think I've been briefed on the entire escapade of the past week. How much money are you going to be transferring?"

"The banker at Zurich Swiss One told us 570 million euros," I said carefully. Tusk sighed deeply and nodded.

"That is… a lot of money. I will refer you to the Minister of Finances," he pulled a notepad out from a drawer beneath the table and scribbled a name and phone number. "He can coordinate the transmission of funds."

"Thank you, sir," I said.

"I'm just curious," Tusk said as he ripped the page of the notepad out and handed it to me. "You stole the money from Kalinka, you didn't need to give it back to the government. Why didn't you take it and run with it? You wouldn't need to work another day of your life."

I didn't think I'd be asked that question, much less by the prime minister. I had always known that the money wouldn't stay with me, though, and I knew the exact reason why.

"It is for a debt that needed to be paid for transgressions of the past," I said, standing up from the table. The clock on the wall indicated that our fifteen minutes were coming to a close.

"Your honor, Miss Sosna, is exceptional. Your family would be proud."

Tusk stood up and took us to the door of the conference room, where his secretary waited outside to receive us. We shook hands and departed towards the lobby, leaving behind the last and most highly ranked member of the government we would potentially ever meet.

~ ~ ~

We departed the Chancellery and headed to our last appointment we had scheduled in Poland before our flight back to Chicago the next day. I insisted that I needed to see Agata one more time to tie up loose ends. She deserved to know what happened to her husband.

"Cousin!" Agata exclaimed, standing from the café table as we entered a small restaurant in Wola. We greeted Agata with a kiss on each cheek, then sat down across from her at the marble-top table, ordering cappuccinos right away from the waitress.

"Tell me all about your travels. I know you've been involved somehow with the headlines. The name Kalinka is on every tongue this week," Agata whispered. She was completely absorbed by the news and ready to hear everything we had to say, but there was still a noticeable sadness in her tone.

"Let's start with you," I said. "Did you ever hear anything more about Marek?"

Agata stared at me, then swallowed and cleared her throat before speaking carefully.

"His body was found in the Vistula River," Agata whispered. She grabbed at her glass of water on the table. I reached across the table to take her by the hand.

"Agata…"

"I know he wasn't an honest person, Joanna," she responded preemptively. "I don't think he was working in the interest of Poland."

"Why do you say that?" Emil asked, sounding as surprised as I was that she perhaps already knew of Marek's involvement with Kalinka.

"The timing with the headlines this week, his absence from home saying he was 'working' even after he started with the Ministry of Transportation, how fast he was able to get you the guns to take to the tripoint… it didn't seem to fit."

I looked at Emil, weighing in my head whether we should give her any more detail on her husband.

"You last saw him in Suwałki, right? After Emil had been shot?" Agata asked before we had time to speak.

"Yes. He came to check on me."

"And then he never came home," Agata stated in her matter-of-fact tone. "I'll bury him, and I'll mourn him. The dead deserve to be remembered. We are not all saints, at the end of the day. He just didn't have time to fix his ways before he died."

Marek was the misfit of our eventful tour of Europe. He gave us our firearms, then killed our ally. He provided information about Kalinka but withheld that he had been working for her. He stood, it seemed, with one foot on either side of the line that divided right from wrong, justice from comfort.

In reviewing his actions, however, another thought, perhaps one that would offer my cousin some closure, dawned on me. I interrupted Emil and Agata's conversation they were carrying on while I was pondering the thought.

"Agata, we think Marek was killed because Kalinka found out he hadn't carried out an assassination of an individual who provided information on her organization's activity," I started. Emil and Agata paused to look at me.

"Marek killed Magda. And he tried to kill Janina. That was his mistake," Emil said, sipping the coffee he had ordered.

"Are you sure it was a mistake?" I asked.

I let the suggestion sink in as I watched Emil's eyes dart across the café table, latching on to my analysis of Marek.

"We're so quick to judge and to resist naivete that we often don't stop to consider someone's good intentions," I added, assisting in Emil's thought process.

"He left Janina there for us to find," Emil said. "He wasn't playing us. He was playing Kalinka. That's why he didn't want to bring this to the SKW. He wasn't scared that they'd react brashly and send us into a war with Russia. He knew that they were working for Kalinka, too."

An inner light seemed to flicker behind Agata's eyes. The man she had been married to wasn't a fraud, like we had all assumed. He was our missing link. He was the person who set us all up to take down the enemy, and he hadn't divulged anything to us about his double agency with Kalinka in case we jumped to conclusions and killed him, too.

"He sacrificed himself for you." Agata clarified, her voice breaking. "Kalinka wasn't his to kill. She was yours."

"And he gave his life for me to have that opportunity after what she had done to my family. The circle of history, now finally closed," I said.

"Redeemed," Agata concluded. The smallest smile crept across her face as she set down her cup of coffee and pulled Marek's old box of menthols out of her coat pocket. She set the box on the table while she dug in her purse for her late husband's leftover matches.

"Cigarette?"

30

Emil and I barely had a single bag to pack for the return flight to Chicago the next day. We bought a carry-on sized weekender at a travel boutique on Nowy Świat and stuffed it with crumpled pieces of newspaper to cushion the three bottles of moonshine vodka that Janina gave to us in Suwałki to bring home.

As we tore pages from that morning's newspaper to push into the leather bag, I read the headlines in Polish:

COLD WAR-ERA RUSSIAN CRIMINAL ORGANIZATION DISCOVERED AND DISBANDED.

EXPLOSION IN LITHUANIAN FOREST. FOUR DEAD.

NATION IN MOURNING AS PRESIDENTIAL FUNERAL APPROACHES.

NUCLEAR RODS FROM TR-003 POWER PLANT SAFELY RETURNED.

KALINKA: MERCILESS MOBSTER, SOVIET SCOUNDREL.

RIOTS AT PARLIAMENTARY BUILDING CEASE AFTER DAYS OF DESTRUCTION.

Poland was perturbed but was slowly settling and returning to its state of equilibrium. It was a liberation that hadn't been enjoyed since before the communist period, since the few moments of freedom in the lull between world wars when she was a republic, free from the chains of her oppressing neighbors. She had now entered a new era, one without the paranoia of subjection, one stripped of the corruption that had existed for seven decades. This was the Poland for which Dziadek, Magda, Wujek, the Polish underground, the Wachlarz movement, and the Damned Soldiers fought and died. This was, I thought, how they were finally redeemed and resting in the peace of their nation's emancipation.

~ ~ ~

We landed at O'Hare and, despite our protests, were picked up late in the evening from the airport by Wujek and Helena.

"How was I supposed to sit at home waiting for you to come visit me, knowing you were already in Chicago? The headlines have been sensational! No, I had to drive to you and see you as soon as possible. You must tell me everything," Wujek asserted as we drove away from the international terminal.

We spent the evening at his small house on the northside, eating a dinner effortlessly composed by Helena and letting him enthusiastically dissect the events of our trip on our behalf. He was amused, astounded, and enthralled all at once, standing up at various points of the conversation to reenact how he thought the scene would have looked. Helena smiled and quietly set plates of different courses before us, starting with a mushroom soup and ending with a homemade poppyseed cake.

"We did bring you a gift," Emil said after Wujek had exhausted all of his questions. He unzipped the weekender and pulled out one of the three bottles of vodka that Janina had gifted. He set the bottle on the table in front of Wujek.

"No Żubrówka?" Wujek asked shyly, pulling the bottle closer towards him and inspecting its clear contents.

"It's even better, we guarantee it," I said, laughing. He still didn't know he could buy his favorite bison grass vodka at the Polish liquor store down the street.

"And I have a gift for you," Wujek said. He stood up from his kitchen chair and went to a cabinet, pulling out an envelope. He slowly made his way back to the table where we sat and set the envelope in front of me.

"The funeral home called me, since you left the country in such a rush, and wanted to return your grandfather's personal possessions following the funeral. You never picked them up."

"What is it?" I took the envelope and tore the seal open.

"I have his clothes and watch in the other room, but they also found this note with his belongings. They say that usually when a person dies with a note on them, it can be significant."

I pulled a folded piece of paper out of the envelope and read the words, written in his shaky but elegant cursive, out loud to Wujek, Helena, and Emil.

> *"In this life, I've hidden things, my doll,*
> *And by now, perhaps you've discovered it all,*
> *That a life in this country, or a life overseas,*
> *Could never put this restless heart at ease.*

With one thing, though, you can rest assured:

The last weapons you searched for were never secured.

The weapons, instead are our weaknesses, our flaws,

When we put our pride above the laws.

Above the highest nations, above the highest gods,

Are where the arrogant, the greedy, the criminals, the frauds

All place themselves, instead of in the shadow

With the servants, the humble, the soldiers below.

Sacrifice and martyrdom and passion and blood

Are what these servants pay, caked in the mud

Of being trampled beneath the feet of the esteemed.

And if you walk with the servants, you die, but redeemed.

Fear not death, it is certain. If you've lived wise,

My doll, my granddaughter, my hope, you will rise."

I set the paper down, my hands trembling and hot tears streaming down my face.

"My God, girl, are you alright?" Wujek asked in his boisterous, booming voice. He set his wrinkled hand on my arm. "It's just that I've never seen you cry."

"The warheads never existed," Emil said in disbelief. I shook my head in agreement. "He just wanted to delude his enemies."

I didn't cry because of the relief that we hadn't left three nuclear warheads hidden around Russia. I cried from the searing wisdom of my grandfather's words that penetrated me even from his grave. He had been ill, but even his sickness couldn't prevent him from writing with clarity and confidence. He remembered me. He remembered his past. He remembered his failures. He remembered his dignity. He wasn't perfect, but he knew the code he should have lived by. And in his missteps, he demonstrated to me how I needed to live. I followed his example and, without even intending it, freed him from his sorrows of the past.

Wujek, still shocked by my reaction to the poem I read, fumbled with the cap to the bottle of vodka from Janina.

"Helena, *podaj kieliszki*," he whispered sharply at his wife, demanding she bring over shot glasses. Four glasses were arranged on the table, filled to the brim, and raised by each of us.

"To Colonel Henryk Jerzy Sosna, to the Damned Soldiers, to your life and your love," Wujek toasted, motioning to me and Emil. "And to all those who have finally been freed."

Epilogue

Emil's flight back to Boston was departing in two hours. He was showered, packed, and sitting on his grandfather's sunken leather couch in front of the television that was blaring a Polish soap opera about a woman catching her husband having an affair with the town's grocer in the back of a car behind a church. Wujek and Helena were so locked into the show that I wondered if they had just discovered what television was.

"Ready?" I asked, closing my phone after having scrolled through my most recent work emails. I was back to reality, and power of attorney forms, wire transfer authorizations, and new mining contracts needed to be signed as soon as possible. A sadness crept over me as I realized that Emil would be half a country away again, leaving me in Chicago.

"Yes," Emil said, standing up from the couch.

"Where are your bags?" Wujek asked, his eyes still glued to the television.

"They're right on the floor, Wujek," I replied, starting for the front door.

"Not his bags," Wujek clarified, finally turning his face away from the screen. He took the remote and turned down the volume. "Yours."

"Dziadek…" Emil whispered.

"What are you talking about?" I asked.

"Let's just go to the airport," Emil said, taking my arm.

"I'm not going with him to Boston, Wujek," I said as Emil nudged me away from his grandparents.

"I know you're not going to Boston. I meant back to Poland."

I whipped my head in Emil's direction, confused by the entire exchange, demanding an explanation with my furrowed eyebrows. Emil dropped his hand from my arm.

"Where are you going?" I asked Emil.

"I'm going back to Poland. With you."

"Why?" My palms started sweating as I waited for him to clear up my disorientation.

"Because I think I've finally decided to become less busy in Boston," Emil said. "I called my realtor and have a purchase pending on a condo in Kraków, Joanna. For us."

My knees quivered and the shaking reverberated down to my feet, which became weak as I stood in that living room in my heels, facing the only man I knew I wanted to be with. I was at a loss for words as he revealed to me that he wanted the same with me.

It was the invisible that I finally realized spoke loudest to me. It was quiet acts of affection, in the living room of an elderly couple with a television that still played too loudly. It was forgotten sacrifices of the past, drowned out by momentous occasions of glory written into textbooks and on classroom blackboards. And it was the words of the dead, sung silently from the grave of history, waiting to be heard. It was easier to let these slip from memory than to cling to them for their humble strength. Only when we clung to them could they be remembered, and only when we remembered them could they be learned.

I had half an hour to return to my condo, pack my bag, take my passport, and make it to O'Hare in time to catch that afternoon's flight, this time to Kraków.

I returned to a free Poland, as Dziadek did in 1989 after communism fell, but now, it was Kalinka that had collapsed. I didn't think I'd be able to tell the difference, having just left the same country two days before. It might have been the feeling of that first cigarette I shared with Emil on the balcony of our new condo, overlooking a city that was over eight hundred years old. Or it might have been the vindication of destroying the tunnel at the tripoint and all the malevolence we brought down with it.

Either way, freedom was in the air, and we indulged in it the entire night as we watched our smoke rise above the ancient rooftops, sovereign once more.

Acknowledgements

A special thanks to my loving family for giving me the time, space, and support I needed to finish *The Tripoint*. You know me best of all, and you know that I love starting countless projects before I finish one. I'm proud to say that I've finished this one, though, and that you helped me through it.

Thank you to all my friends and family who reviewed this book prior to self-publishing. Your feedback and time spent with me on *The Tripoint* is priceless.

Finally, thank you to my ancestors who taught me the value of honor, discipline, and hope. Many of these people are now deceased – Dziadek Jurek, Babcia Zosia, Ciocia Mela, Babcia Wacia, Ciocia Basia, and Daddy – but their legacies remain. Without your sacrifices, there would be no story to write.

About the Author

Julia Sophia Banasikowski Weir was born to a Polish immigrant family in White Plains, New York in 1993. She was raised in the Polish community of Northeast Minneapolis, attending Polish school every Saturday for thirteen years and performing with a Polish folk song and dance ensemble, which traveled Europe. Throughout high school, she also participated in various international historical competitions, primarily through the Warsaw-based Institute of National Remembrance, which strengthened her awareness of Poland's agonizing 20th century history.

Julia studied at the University of Notre Dame and graduated in 2015 with a degree in Accountancy and a minor in European Studies. While on campus, she became well acquainted with the Nanovic Institute for European Studies and earned a monetary grant to travel to Warsaw to conduct research on the 1940 Katyń Massacre, a war crime perpetrated on Poles by the Soviets during World War II. Her thesis project went on to win various university awards, including the

Robert J. Wegs Prize and Honorable Mention at the Undergraduate Library Research Awards.

Her studies of Polish history at the University of Notre Dame deepened her respect for her ancestors' fatherland. She remains active in broadening her knowledge about Polish history and its impact on current events. In 2020, she received the Polish-American Award from the Polonia Institute in California for her essay on how Russia can be held accountable for the 1940 Katyń Massacre.

Julia has been freelance writing for two years since graduation with articles appearing, both internationally and domestically, in publications such as the Paris-based Eastern European Film Bulletin and the University of Notre Dame's Grotto Network.

At the age of 27 years old, Julia works fulltime as an accounting manager for a Fortune 10 company. She currently lives with her husband and two sons in a suburb of Minneapolis, near her mother and sister.

Made in the USA
Coppell, TX
01 October 2021